ENFORCER UNLEASHED

Feral Pack: Book Three

EVE LANGLAIS

PROLOGUE

THE FOREST WHIPPED BY IN A GREEN AND BROWN blur as he ran, his four furry feet finding purchase on the loamy ground. He panted, the hotness of it puffing in the cooler air. His heart raced as he moved quickly and quietly. Try as he might, he couldn't escape the distant baying of the hounds.

Don't get caught. He'd seen what happened to those who stumbled. He was the last of his litter after all.

Branches snagged at his fur, the red of it bright against the foliage all around. Matted in spots, he'd not properly groomed since being placed in the tiny cage. A cage too small to stretch in.

The lack of movement and exercise could be felt in his trembling muscles. He wanted nothing more than to stop. Breathe. Rest.

Instead, he had to run faster. Forget hiding, the tracking dogs would sniff him out, and then there'd be no hope of saving himself.

Bursting out of the woods into a clearing, which under different circumstances would have been pretty with its patch of wildflowers growing in the bright sun, he stumbled and plowed into the grass muzzle first as he tried to halt his momentum.

A gangly kit, he could only push back to four feet and try not to shake too hard at the sight of the person standing before him. A female by scent, the fur atop her head silvery and lush. Her eyes captivated with their strange kaleidoscope of colors.

No words were spoken, and yet, when she tilted her head, he understood. *Get behind.*

Why? He didn't understand why a stranger would offer her body as a shield, but he was old enough to grasp she didn't appear to mean him any harm, unlike the dogs and their masters.

He slunk around to the rear of the woman and eyed the edge of the forest on the other side. Should he run for it while she appeared distracted?

His ears pricked as a hound bayed. Close. So very close now.

A low, growling rumble had him glancing at the woman again as she stepped forward. Unafraid of the approaching dogs. She didn't know of the hunters who followed them.

He yipped.

She glanced at him over her shoulder. "Fear not, little kit," she whispered.

He gave another short bark that he hoped she understood as a warning. *Danger.*

She winked and bared her teeth in a wicked smile. It oddly reassured.

As the first of the dogs emerged into the clearing, she uttered a single piercing whistle that almost made him howl.

He watched with wide eyes as she charged the hounds that had been tracking him. With long strides, she headed for the barking dogs, ignoring the fact they outnumbered her five to one.

Probably because she wasn't attacking alone.

A pair of wolves emerged from the forest, a brindle and one so dark he'd be invisible at night. The sight of them proved enough to have the dogs tucking their tails and retreating in the direction they'd come from, wailing in fear.

The pair of newcomer wolves followed the hounds, but the silvery-haired female paused and turned back to eye him. "It's safe now. You don't have to hide anymore."

In that moment he understood, *She's like me.*

The knowledge had him shifting into his other shape, the two-legged one with spindly legs and soft belly. He didn't often change, because his cage couldn't accommodate his other side. His floppy red hair fell in his face, partially covering his eyes.

Expression soft, she smiled at him and held out her hand. "Come with me, my special little kit. It's time to take you somewhere safe. A place where you can thrive and grow."

He understood her words even though he didn't speak. Apprehension beset him. Who was she? What did she want?

He heard a sharp, yelping cry of pain and snarls as the wolves clashed with the hounds. Hounds that would have hurt him if he'd been caught.

"I promise, I don't want to harm you. No one will ever harm you, or they will answer to me," she added in a low growl. "You have my word as an emissary of the Lykosium."

While not used to kindness, he craved it. Something about this female asked him to trust. He clasped her outstretched fingers.

The woman, called Luna, took him home with her, raised him, protected him, and taught him to fight for himself.

When he hit manhood, and the opportunity

presented itself, he paid back Luna's generosity by serving her and, in the process, saved other Were from the fate he'd almost suffered.

And like those who'd hunted him and his kind, Kit showed no mercy.

ONE

"When are you returning?" Luna asked, her right as Kit's superior and current head of the Lykosium Council. She was also his foster mother, but not when it came to council business.

Kit transferred the phone to his other ear before replying, "Soon. My investigation here isn't quite done." As a Lykosium enforcer, who also acted as a spy, Kit was one of the trusted few who ensured the Were Packs followed the rules, and if they didn't, he brought them in for justice, or meted it out, depending on the circumstances.

"Oh?" Nothing else, just that simple word. Growing up, he'd known Luna not to be the type to ask many questions or force answers. It had proved oddly effective.

"I've got a lead." Not much of one, and yet, it gnawed at his gut.

"Do you, or are you letting your emotions cloud your judgment?"

"That would be a first," was his dry reply. His early childhood as a hunting toy for sadistic humans had left its mark. He didn't trust easily, Luna being one of the few he truly cared for. He owed his life to her—and his dumb name. How original, naming a Were with impossible fox genetics Kit. In her defense, when she'd found him as a toddler, he'd had no name. No words. Nothing but an instinct for survival.

"This is about that girl," Luna stated.

No need for a name, because *she* filled his mind.

Poppy Smith. Not her real name. Born Penelope Moondust Jameson, she was six years younger than Kit—not that age mattered.

He'd first come across her when on the trail of a Were gone feral. Kit had tracked Samuel, a former Alpha with abusive tendencies, to a remote ranch in Northern Alberta. He'd ended up finding more than he'd expected, including a woman who flinched at shadows.

As someone who'd once done the same, he'd recognized the signs of abuse. That had led to him investigating those living at the ranch, seeking a culprit, only to realize her fear resulted from abuse in her past. That should have been the end of it. Instead, he'd looked deeper. Once he'd started, the mystery had deepened.

"This isn't about Ms. Smith but rather her former Pack. It's my belief something unnatural happened to them." Something that to this day caused Poppy to have night terrors. He'd heard her crying out. Not that he was stalking her, just doing his regular enforcer thing.

"If you think it merits further investigation, then you have my blessing."

As if there could be any other outcome.

"Thanks." He hung up and pondered his next move.

He had few options, given the Pack Penelope/Poppy used to belong to had disbanded quite a few years back. Already small in size, it had been decimated by a spate of accidental deaths, including that of the Alpha. The few left had scattered, including Penelope.

She hadn't resurfaced until the return of her brother. Darian, her only sibling, had taken leave from the military to visit family, only to then request a discharge, citing personal issues, namely his mother's death in a hunting accident. Which happened more than it should among the Were. It took only one bullet to end a life.

There existed a distinct possibility that Darian had abandoned his career to care for his younger sister. It didn't explain the part where they'd disappeared, leaving behind no clue as to where or why. They'd not just relocated but changed their names and ended up in the most remote of locations.

Smelled like a secret to Kit.

Whatever the reason for their actions, he'd wager it had to do with why Poppy locked the doors even in this remote place. Explained why she jumped at the crack of a branch and her whimpers at night when a nightmare shook her.

What he didn't understand? Why it bothered him. He'd found himself intrigued from the moment he'd seen her, a fragile-looking beauty, her hair a light brown, long and straight, her frame in need of a few more pounds to remove the gauntness. Ironically, she cooked. A lot. Judging by the expressions and exclamations of those she fed, she knew her stuff, even as she barely picked at her own meals.

He couldn't blame the decadent aroma of her beef stew or the mouthwatering temptation of her apple pie for his obsession. His fascination with her began the first time he'd caught her lingering scent in the vegetable garden.

The most perfect aroma. It teased. Tempted. Made him want to get close.

A part of him understood why. The mating instinct. Not a thing he'd ever expected to experience, given he was only half Were. Yet, there was no denying he was drawn to Poppy. Also repelled, because he had no intention of ever settling down with anyone.

He hadn't dug into her past because of his interest in her but because he'd been trained to sniff out danger. Something about her Pack and her situation didn't smell right.

For one, Packs didn't just disband. That required heavy attrition or tragedy. In this case, more than seven members had gone missing in a short period of time. As in gone without taking any of their things with them.

Their departure hadn't gone unnoticed. However, the police had no leads at the time, and it hadn't helped that no one filed any missing-person reports. Just like no one noticed when Penelope suddenly stopped attending her college culinary classes. She'd gone from getting almost-perfect grades to not showing up. And no one thought to find out why.

The why led to him diving deeper. He'd found more than expected. Poppy's mother, Kora Jameson, only had the two kids. Her husband died when they were young. Some kind of construction incident. She'd never remarried and lived in the same house until selling it a year before her new place burned down—with her and her boyfriend of the time in it. Records showed the place being owned by a company renting to a Gerard Kline, a very wealthy man.

And that was all Kit could find on the man. No history, no pictures, nothing. He supposedly had died in the fire, too, not that his body was found, just Kora's. The fire was ruled an accident—something about a nest in the chimney.

In a stroke of even worse luck, while Penelope Jameson had been fleeing the burning house, she'd been accidentally shot by what police assumed was a hunter. Had her brother not arrived to visit at just that very moment and provided first aid, she might not have survived. The hospital report listed extensive injuries, some that seemed to have little to do with gunshot wounds to her leg and in the gut.

The police hadn't considered Penelope and her brother lucky and spent much time questioning the pair about the fire and the deaths of their mother and her boyfriend. In the end, they had nothing to charge them with, no sign of foul play.

When the hospital eventually released Penelope, she disappeared with her brother. And that should have been the end of it. Only...

Recently, it had been brought to the attention of the Lykosium that a local Pack had been losing members. More than a dozen now, although some had fled on their own.

Those few had taken all their shit with them. The others? They'd left food rotting in fridges, abandoned their bank accounts, and simply vanished.

It reminded him of Penelope's Pack. And wouldn't you know it? The same company that had rented a house to Gerard Kline was now leasing one to a Theodore Kline.

Coincidence? Kit didn't believe in them. He had to wonder if perhaps there was a reason no one had found a body in that fire. A reason why a certain young woman had appeared, abused and traumatized, in the hospital, many of her injuries not caused by a fire or gunshot wounds.

Hypothesizing that this Kline person might be hurting the Were and acting on those suspicions, though, were two different things. Kit might be ruthless, but he also stringently followed the Lykosium rules imposed on him. There could be no sentencing without proof, which he wouldn't get while hanging around the ranch. He'd finished his task here. The feral Samuel had been taken care of. The illegal number of Were gathered at the ranch had been given legal Pack status. The job was done.

But he couldn't leave yet.

He had one thing left to do.

TWO

Poppy glanced out the kitchen window of the ranch house for the third time in the last hour. The garden remained the same—green, growing and empty. Despite that, the nagging sense of being watched lingered, putting her on edge.

Ever since the episode with Samuel, and the Lykosium, she'd been fidgety and nervous. She'd never even known the ranch was being watched. Did someone still spy?

Why would they? They weren't doing anything wrong. Just living and farming as a real Pack now, with an Alpha who cared for them.

Realistically, Poppy understood she had no reason to worry. No one here would hurt her, and all would stand as a shield in front of her if she required aid. Knowing that didn't help with her increasing anxiety, though, and the return of her nightmares.

She couldn't even pinpoint what triggered their resurgence, yet she couldn't ignore the results. She woke whimpering, sweaty and embarrassed. Then she felt horrible because her night terrors also woke her brother, who then soothed her while trying to hide his rage and impotence that he couldn't fix this for her.

Darian had always been the big brother who made bad things go away.

When a kid had pushed Poppy at the playground and sent her home sobbing with a scraped knee, the bully had shown up the next day with two bandaged knees and an apology.

The boy who dumped her for another girl? Said girl ditched the boy because a handsome senior asked her out.

Her big brother had always been there for Poppy, except when he wasn't. He'd joined the military fresh out of high school, and that would have been fine had their mother not gotten involved with the wrong sort.

Poppy blinked and ducked her head. *Nope. Nope. Not going there.* Some things were best left in the past.

She busied herself prepping dinner for the

massive gang living at the ranch. Astra was ready to give birth any day now and had a hovering hubby named Bellamy. Then there were Pierce, Reece, Nova, Hammer, the grumpy Lochlan, and the Alpha of Feral Pack, Amarok, with his new wife, Meadow. They'd recently lost someone, Asher, their resident jokester, when he'd moved to the city to be with his mate, but he kept in touch. While she was happy he'd found love, she missed his easygoing smile and humor.

The food Poppy put out got devoured and declared delicious. Nothing new. They said that about every meal. Since she cooked, everyone else pitched in to do cleanup, except for Astra, who had her feet up and a hand on her jiggling belly.

"I think the baby liked the sugar pie," Astra said with a smile at her bulging midsection.

In the beginning of the pregnancy, Poppy had envied her friend. As a young girl, she'd always imagined herself with several kids. Then that option was taken away from her. The best she could hope for was to live vicariously through others.

"Do you want me to make you an herbal tea?" she offered.

"No more liquids!" Astra groaned. "I almost peed myself last night when the baby kicked me in the bladder."

A smile tugged at Poppy's lips. "Won't be long now."

"Don't remind me," Astra said with a mock groan. She and Bellamy couldn't wait to add to their family. They'd had to fight against their families to be together, but they loved each other enough that they'd refused to bow to pressure.

At times, Poppy wished she could find that kind of love, and then the reality of her past hit. No man would ever want her once he knew the truth.

"I think I'm going to crash early," she said, noticing it was already dark outside except for the solar lights that provided a bright path from the ranch to the cabin she shared with her brother. They'd installed them just for her so she wouldn't have to traverse the path in the dark. She'd never told them that the lights made her anxiety worse, because they deepened the shadows beyond the lit path.

To leave, she had to go through the kitchen and run the gauntlet of well-meaning people. *Are you okay? Do you want company? How about I walk you?*

She turned them all down and said, "Just tired. I'm going to stuff my face with treats and read a book in bed." To back up her statement, she grabbed a tin of freshly baked cookies and smiled as she went out the back door.

Walking the path, she wondered if anyone

watched. It took effort to not run. If she did, someone might see and demand to know why. She could never tell. Bad enough that they all treated her like a wounded animal. If they truly understood—

She shook her head, chasing the thoughts that wouldn't stop. Why now? Why, after all this time, did the memories keep trying to surface? *Stay in your box.* She kept that box locked when she was awake, but it kept sneaking open when she slept.

She entered the cabin, and the cookie tin she held almost hit the floor when she realized she wasn't alone.

Her heart hammered, and she fought to not tremble. "What are you doing here?" she asked of the man sitting in her brother's favorite chair, the bright red of his hair a contrast to his cold gaze. She set the container of treats down before she dropped it.

"We meet again."

"Hardly 'again,' since we didn't speak the last time." But she remembered seeing him at a warehouse when Asher had rescued Val from some bad people and she'd swallowed her fear and gone along to help.

Kit. No last name. A Lykosium enforcer. Here in her house.

She tried to not shake too hard and fought to keep a quiver from her voice. "What do you want?"

"Your help." A flat statement.

"With?" She dug her fingers into her palms, fearing his next words.

His lips held a sly curve, and her stomach dropped as he purred, "Take a guess why the Lykosium might require your services specifically, Penelope Moondust Jameson."

The use of her old name chilled her. She shook her head and hugged herself. "You have the wrong person."

"Don't waste your breath lying. I know who you are. I know where you come from. And I need your help."

He could be asking only one thing of her. The one thing she couldn't do. "I can't."

"Who says you have a choice? The Lykosium are calling upon you to aid in an investigation involving crimes against the Were."

Her lips quivered as she whispered, "I'd rather die."

"As well as condemn others, apparently."

"I can't help you." She clenched her hands into tight fists, digging her nails into her palms, trying to stem the tremors as he reminded her of why she'd fled to what some considered the edge of the world.

"You can. If you stop wallowing in fear."

Her chin lifted. "It's called self-preservation."

"Is that what we're calling cowardice these days?"

The insult dropped her jaw. "Get out."

"I'll leave, but only because I'm done here. You have the night to think it over." Kit stood suddenly, too tall and imposing. Not a friend like Amarok and the others.

"I don't need time to know the past should remain buried." Because, like bodies, the past stank only more with age.

He stared at her long enough she shivered. Mostly in fear, but also in awareness. The scent of him. The breadth. The strength.

"Is it buried, though? Because it seems to me you're living with it every day." And with that ominously perceptive statement, he left. It was only then she noticed that he'd left behind a faint whiff of fox and a certainty that had her swallowing hard.

I think he might be my mate.

Not that she'd ever find out for sure. The very reason he'd come to her for help was the thing that ensured someone broken like her, tainted and imperfect, could never find love.

I'm not worthy.

THREE

She's my mate.

It shouldn't have been possible, not for someone unworthy like Kit. Not on account of anything he'd done but because of pure genetics. Kit was what some called an impossibility. A Were fox with some wolf traits. No one knew how it had happened, but Kit had some theories, none of them pleasant.

As Kit slipped out of the cabin through the rear door, he paused as he realized someone waited for him.

"What the fuck are you doing here?" Darian, Poppy's older brother, emerged from the shadows, fists clenched at his sides, expression tight with anger —and fear. Even Were with nothing to hide showed caution when a Lykosium-sanctioned enforcer showed up on their doorstep.

"I had something to discuss with your sister."

"Like fuck!" Kit made no move to defend himself as the other man grabbed and slammed him against the wall of the cabin. "Leave Poppy alone!"

"I'm afraid that's not possible." Not entirely true. Kit could find a way to investigate without using her, and yet, he'd chosen to confront her, hoping to get close enough to assuage his curiosity. It hadn't worked.

"Why?"

"I might have found the one who hurt her."

"He's dead."

"Dead people leave behind bodies," Kit pointed out.

"Are you saying Gerard is alive? Where?" Darian released Kit and clenched his fists, seething.

"Is there a reason you are interested?" Because Kit had yet to truly discover if the man named Gerard Kline had committed any crimes.

"Fuck yeah, I'm interested. Fucker hurt my mother and sister."

Oddly, the confirmation didn't give Kit relief, igniting his own ire instead. "You're sure of that? Your sister will confirm?"

"No, she's not confirming, because you better not have told her Gerard might not be dead."

"Surely she suspects."

Darian whirled and punched the nearest thing, which happened to be a tree trunk. "Yes, she suspects. Fuck. I should have gone in after that fucker to make sure he was dead." Darian slewed a dark expression in his direction. "Where is he?"

"I'm afraid I can't tell you, especially since I can't be sure if he is the same man."

"Was Poppy unable to identify him?" Darian glanced at the cabin.

"I have nothing to show, because the images I've managed to acquire haven't been of the best quality. The suspect is rather camera-shy. I'm afraid a more direct approach might be needed."

Understanding dawned, and Darian shook his head. "No. You are not getting her near that monster. Hasn't she suffered enough?" His anger also held sorrow—and guilt because he'd not protected her.

"Others might still be suffering."

"Then do something about it."

"It's not that simple."

Darian leaned close. "It's called a bullet to the head. If you won't do it, then tell me where the bastard is hiding, and I'll handle it."

"Like you did the last time? You set the fire, didn't you?"

"He barricaded himself in the house. It was the only option I had."

"And it failed because Gerard Kline appears to have escaped."

"You think I'm not aware of that? At the time, I thought he'd die. I'd shot him. Set fire to the house."

"With your mother inside?"

Darian's face darkened. "She was already dead."

"You thought that of Kline, too. Perhaps you should have stayed to watch your handiwork."

"I couldn't. Poppy needed me."

"You didn't wait to ensure the job was done, which is why I'm here."

"You are not using my sister. I won't allow it. Find someone else."

"There is no one else. She's the only one alive who's seen and scented him, who might be able to identify our subject of interest."

The argument didn't help. Darian snapped, "You want to put her in danger."

"I wouldn't allow her to be harmed. If she agrees, I plan to be her shadow every step of the way."

"What if you miscalculate? What if it is Gerard and he gets his hands on her and hides her?"

"There is technology to ensure that can't happen."

Repugnance curled Darian's lip. "You want to chip her."

"It's the best way to make sure she's not lost."

"She won't get lost because she's not going anywhere with you." Darian spoke firmly.

"That's not your choice to make."

"Fuck yeah, it is. That's my baby sister. And I might have failed her once, but I won't fail her again."

Kit didn't fault Darian for his protectiveness. Kit could even continue his investigation without Poppy. However, he couldn't walk away, because he understood Poppy better than Darian did. "How are her nightmares?" he asked, shifting the conversation.

"How do you know about those?"

"You really have to ask?"

Darian rubbed his face. "Of course. You know because you've been spying."

"Don't you want to give her a chance to stop them? To stop living in fear, always looking over her shoulder?"

"Kill the fucker who abused her, and maybe she'll feel safe."

"Will she? Or does she need closure? A way of fighting back?"

"What she needs is to not be reminded."

"According to you. Maybe you should talk to her and see what she says." He glanced at the window, where the curtain twitched.

When Darian's gaze followed, Kit made his exit,

blending into the shadows, aware Poppy had heard every word.

Despite what he'd said to Darian, and her, the final choice to help or not was hers. He'd never force her. Never hurt her.

One way or another, though, he would avenge her.

FOUR

Poppy moved from the window, knowing she'd been caught eavesdropping. Then again, the men hadn't been entirely discreet in their discussion.

She'd heard the whole thing. Darian trying to protect her. Kit sounding cold but, at the same time, making a valid point.

Would acting against the one who'd hurt her ease her anxiety? Then again, what could she do? She'd been powerless in the past. Nothing had changed since then, other than the fact she hid from life now.

Darian stormed inside, his glower softening at the sight of her. "You okay?"

Everyone always asked her that. Treated her with kid gloves. As if she were fragile.

Broken. She was, yet at the same time she wanted to scream to stop treating her as if she were weak. Other times, she wanted to hide behind others and let them be her shield. Was that how she planned to live the rest of her life?

"You shouldn't have been so rude to him," she admonished. "He works for the Lykosium Council."

"Fuck the council. Where were they when you suffered?"

"They didn't know." A soft excuse.

"They should have." He blamed them, but she didn't.

"How could they know when I was never able to tell anyone? They're not omniscient. And it was my fault." She should have seen the signs that Gerard hadn't been who he'd claimed to be.

"It's not your fault!" he vehemently denied. "That man Mom hooked up with was a sick monster."

"I don't want to talk about it." She shut down the conversation because she'd had it too many times before. Darian would yell and bluster then blame himself for enlisting and leaving them. She'd cry. He'd feel bad. Then they'd both pretend everything was okay, ignoring the fact she'd not gotten any better.

While Darian wanted to keep ranting, he didn't push. Because she was delicate.

Ugh. Kit hadn't acted as if she would crumble.

He wanted her help. If only he hadn't asked for the one thing she couldn't do.

When she went to bed, no surprise, the past rose to swamp her.

THE HOUSE they pulled up in front of screamed money. Penelope's eyes widened from her spot in the passenger seat of her mom's car.

"This is where Gerard lives?" Gerard being Mom's new boyfriend.

Mom nodded.

"All this from investing other people's money?" She couldn't help the note of incredulity, because it seemed farfetched even for a girl now in her second year of college.

"He's so smart."

Intelligent and observant, too much so for a human. That first meeting, Gerard charmed her. Spoiled them both with food and entertainment. Before long, they were frequent visitors. It was a good time. A happy time. So, it seemed only natural for Mom to move in with Gerard, with a room set aside for Penelope's personal use. After all, he had plenty of space for them both—including more than a hundred acres of forest to run in. For a Were attending college in the city and stressing about her courses, the times she went to visit proved so relaxing. Every chance she got, Penelope piled her clothes in the bole of a tree and ran four-legged for hours.

This went on for six months before it all changed.

It happened over spring break. Despite not having talked on the phone for a few weeks, she and Mom had been texting constantly. When she arrived, it seemed odd Mom wasn't there to greet her, only Gerard.

"Where's Mom?" she asked as she lugged her suitcase up the steps as the cab drove off.

"Resting. She's been feeling poorly lately."

"Oh no. Why didn't she say anything?" she exclaimed.

"Didn't want you worrying. Besides, in her condition, it's perfectly normal."

"Condition?" she repeated on a querying note. "Is she sick?"

"Yes. With the morning kind." Gerard beamed. "We're pregnant."

"Oh." The surprise hit her, especially since Mom, in her late forties, had always said she was done having kids.

"You're going to be a big sister."

"That's great!" The excitement wasn't entirely feigned. She loved babies. "When can I see her?"

"Soon. First, I need to show you something. Something special I made just for you."

He led her to the lower level, a place she'd never been, given the massive house had everything she needed. She expected a recreation room. Perhaps even a bowling alley, a thing popular with the rich.

Instead, they passed through a thick wooden door into a sterile space with metal counters and medical equipment. Before she could whirl and ask where they were, a pinprick in her arm had her blacking out.

She woke in a cage. A cage that was big enough she could stand and rattle the bars, screaming herself hoarse.

What happened? Why was she being imprisoned?

Her mother was the one to reveal those answers. She appeared in the basement, her once-healthy features gaunt, in contrast to her burgeoning belly.

"Mom?" Penelope couldn't help the quaver.

"Oh, my little Poppy Seed. I wish you'd stayed away." Mom broke into tears.

Penelope clutched the bars. "Mom, what's happening?"

"I did this. It's my fault," her mother sobbed. "He told me you'd be left alone if I listened. And I did. Mostly. But then I found out what he did, and I tried to leave..." Her mother couldn't speak for the crying.

Penelope didn't understand. She had to speak

firmly, more firmly than she ever had with her mother. "What's going on? What has Gerard done?"

Her mother couldn't tell her that day, because the man himself arrived and didn't have to say a word. Mom scurried off, and Poppy found out all too soon the depravity he was capable of.

It lasted months. Months where she wanted to die rather than suffer.

Mom, whom she'd not seen since that first day of captivity, was the one to help her escape.

She appeared in the basement, wearing only a filmy robe that did nothing to hide the bruises on her body or the bloodstains running down her legs and on her hands. She had a wild expression on her face and rambled incoherently.

"Quick, quick, before the hunter returns. Run. Run. Faster than a rabbit."

While appearing unhinged, her mother had had the sense to bring the keys that unlocked the cage. Exiting, Penelope grasped her mother's hands.

"What's going on, Mom? Where's Gerard?"

"Dead? For now? Maybe not?" Her mother giggled, a high-pitched, insane sound that tore at Penelope.

"Did you kill him?"

"I tried. So many times. But he just won't die," her mother wailed.

"Let's go." Gerard being dead or alive was of less importance than escape. Together, they made it out of the basement, through the back door, to the edge of the woods.

They went no farther. A gunshot cracked the air, and Mom didn't make a sound. She simply fell to the ground.

"Mom!" Penelope screamed as she saw the blood. Then she screamed again as a second bullet hit her in the leg.

As she crumpled, she half turned to behold Gerard, his hair standing in spikes, his white shirt bloody, his expression mean and intent. The muzzle of his weapon pointed at her.

"Going somewhere?" he asked with a smirk as he strode toward her.

Forget replying when her mother was possibly dead at her feet. Forget the bruises on her body or the throbbing in her leg from the bleeding hole. Anger and frustration took hold, and she shifted. Before she fully finished changing into a wolf, she leaped, just as he fired again. The bullet hit her in the gut but not before she slammed into Gerard and began biting and tearing.

Despite being human, he fought, pulling out a knife and slashing it hard enough she yelped and shoved away from him. Gerard rose to his feet, bleeding and angry.

She tried to stand but collapsed. He stood over her. "Did you really think you could run away?" he said. "There is nowhere you can hide. How do you think I found you and the other perversions?"

He lifted his arm, and that would have been the end if not for the distraction of an arriving car. She took his inattention as her chance to escape. Closed her ears to the gunshots. Ignored the smell of the smoke.

On three legs, she ran through the woods until she collapsed and then crept under a fallen tree. Weak. Hurting. Ready to die.

Which was where Darian found her.

But the nightmare didn't finish that day.

The doctors did what they could to fix her, which gave her time to establish a story with Darian about what had happened. The cops found Mom's body in the burned shell of Gerard's house, but the man himself? His body was never found.

To this day, she still heard him say, "There is nowhere you can hide."

. . .

THE SCREAMS WERE full-throated as she rose from the nightmare. Tangled in her sheets. Sweating and shaking.

Darian arrived in his boxers, wild-haired and frantic-eyed. "I'm here, Poppy Seed."

He'd never left her side since that moment. But having him close didn't help.

Only one thing might.

Which was probably why her brother howled when she said, "I'm going to help the enforcer."

FIVE

KIT HEARD HER SCREAMING AND WANTED TO GO to her. It almost physically hurt to remain hidden outside. He resorted to punching a tree, enough times his knuckles bruised and skin split. The pain, though, helped him to focus.

He should leave. Now. Tonight.

What was he thinking by involving her? The brother had spoken the truth when he'd said she'd suffered enough. Kit had read the hospital reports that detailed not just the injuries that had brought her in for healing but the older ones that had left their marks.

Scars on her back as if she'd been whipped. Burn marks. Signs of needle use, which he'd wager she'd not injected herself, though the doctors had assumed drug abuse.

Add in the gunshot that had taken her womb and a few feet of her intestine and nicked her spine, no wonder she feared facing the man who'd ruined her life.

Had Kit found the culprit? He couldn't be sure, not without her to confirm, because, while faces could change, a person's unique scent didn't.

But she didn't have to be there in person for that. He could bring back something of the suspect, a personal item, preferably clothing he'd worn. It was his fault, he'd wager, that the nightmare hit her so hard this night.

I'm sorry. He truly was. Before he could take a step, the rear door to her cabin opened, and she peeked out.

"Kit?" She uttered his name softly, tentatively.

He almost didn't reply.

"If you're out there, I've made my decision. I'll help you."

What? The courage it took her to utter those trembling words almost sent him fleeing.

How could he ask this of her? He should leave now.

He stepped into the open, sliding from shadow to shadow until he knew she could sense him.

"You don't have to do this. I'll find another way."

He suddenly found himself trying to talk her out of it.

"We both know you came to me because there is no other option. If I'm the only survivor, then only I can identify him."

"If it's him." He injected doubt.

As Poppy went to step outside, her brother reached for her. She slapped his hand away and moved toward Kit.

"What makes you think it is? The police think he died in the house fire and just wasn't found because of the collapse of the house."

"Do you believe he's dead?"

Her lips flattened. "I know he's not. And if you're asking, it's because you found a clue."

"More like a pattern that is similar to the one your Pack experienced."

"My Pack?" Her tone lilted. "What about it? It disbanded after our Alpha died."

"He was shot."

"Cops ruled it a hunting accident."

"Maybe, or could be he was killed by someone who didn't want him making a stink once Pack members started disappearing without a trace."

Darian joined them with a question. "Wait, if people were disappearing, why has it taken so long for the Lykosium to get involved?"

"For one, we didn't know right away. Once we did notice, there was no one left for us to question."

"Until you found me." Poppy's soft statement. "You said it's happening again to another Pack?"

"Maybe. People are disappearing and not resurfacing elsewhere."

"How many?" Darian asked.

Kit shrugged. "Hard to get an exact number since no one will return our calls."

"If that's the case, how do you know anyone is missing?" Poppy's brow creased.

"Because we do keep track of Were when possible. Most are good about notifying us of their whereabouts, which is what makes the sudden disappearances of so many in a short time frame so odd."

"No accidents?"

Kit shook his head. "Nope. And the culprits are doing a better job of cleaning their tracks this time. Entire households have been wiped out. Houses and apartments emptied. Bank accounts closed. Vehicles disappeared. They just stop showing up for their jobs, and their phones are disconnected."

"What makes you think this is related to the fucker who hurt my sister?"

"I don't know if it is. What I do know is there's a man named Theodore Kline renting a home from the same company Gerard was back when you knew him."

"That's a lot of coincidences," she mused aloud.

"Too many."

"Still don't see why you need Poppy. If you need an expert, then why don't you skulk and spy? It's what you're good at." Darian's sarcasm matched Kit's usual dry tone.

"I would, but Kline, despite living in a residential area, is well guarded. Electrified fencing, security guards, cameras."

"Sounds like a you problem," Darian offered with a smirk.

"Not anymore, now that I've found the key to getting inside." Kit barely ducked the fist Darian swung. But the real sucker-punch was Penelope's expression.

SIX

At Kit's words, Darian predictably lost his shit.

"My sister is not entering some guarded compound on a vague hunch some rich dude is offing Were."

"She wouldn't be harmed."

"Oh, how do you figure that?" Darian snapped in between throwing punches. "You said yourself the place is well guarded."

"It is for someone trying to enter quietly. But if there is evidence of crimes being committed against Were, then I have Lykosium approval to go in and handle it."

"You mean Lykosium permission to kill," Poppy interjected.

Kit offered a short nod, his face an implacable

mask, whereas all of Darian's emotions showed on his face and in the timbre of his voice.

No surprise, the yelling meant they were joined by others of the Pack. Rok, Bellamy, Lochlan, and Hammer emerged from the shadows.

Darian whirled with relief. "Thank fuck you're here. Can you believe what this asshole is trying to do to Poppy?"

"Kit won't be doing anything to her that she doesn't agree to," Rok replied.

"Ha." Darian offered a triumphant smirk. "See, you ginger fuckwad? You can take your plan and shove it."

"That's not your decision," Poppy said quietly. A dead silence followed.

"Er, what?" Darian blinked at her.

"I'm tired of being afraid. I don't want to jump at shadows anymore. I need the nightmares to stop. If that man is Gerard, then I want justice for Mom's death. For what he did to me and others." She lifted her head to stare at Kit. "When Gerard dies, I want him to know I'm responsible, that he might have broken me but, in the end, I won."

"It might not be him," Kit warned.

"No, but you seem pretty sure he's involved in whatever is happening to the Were out there."

He hesitated before nodding.

"Whoever this person is, they have to be stopped."

"It doesn't have to be you," Darian declared.

"No, it doesn't, but I want to help." She lifted her chin. "I'd like it if you came with me."

She didn't ask Kit but saw the tightening of his mouth as Darian said, "Fucking right I'm going."

No surprise, the rest of them volunteered, too, which led to her shaking her head. "Bellamy, you know you can't, not with Astra close to dropping that baby. And, Rok, you're a newlywed and the Alpha. You can't go scampering off on something that doesn't concern you."

"You concern me," was Rok's emphatic reply.

"And I love you for it, but this is something I need to do."

In the end, she agreed to let Lochlan and Hammer join them, mostly because she got a perverse pleasure out of seeing Kit rolling his eyes and sighing a few more times.

He might have all the confidence in the world about keeping her safe, but she didn't know him, no matter what her hormones said about him being her mate. She didn't know if she could trust him, but Darian, Lochlan, and Hammer? She knew they'd go through Hell itself to save her, and she needed that reassurance, because if this truly was Gerard, then she would be facing down her biggest fear.

What if she wasn't strong enough? What if... What if she ended up back in that cage?

As if he'd read her mind, Darian leaned close and said, "I won't let anyone hurt you."

Oddly, though, it was Kit's barked, "For fuck's sake, stop acting like she's going to the gallows. She's stronger than you all give her credit for," that did the most to bolster her resolve.

He thought her strong. She wanted to once again be the girl who didn't fear anything in the world but final exams.

"I'm going, and that's final." Then, while they all argued, she stalked to the main house. If they were going on a road trip, she needed to pack food.

And maybe something sexy, because for the first time in a long while, Poppy felt something.

Alive.

SEVEN

DESPITE KIT'S STATEMENT, HE ACTUALLY HATED himself for having asked her, because now that she'd said yes, they'd be spending more time together.

In close proximity.

With her brother and two men who acted like brothers.

Fuck.

With their plans to leave at dawn, Kit had enough time to retrieve his SUV from where he'd hidden it and call Luna.

"How are things?" she asked. She always answered, no matter the hour. At times, he wondered if Luna ever slept. He'd gotten arrested at sixteen for being rowdy, not to mention underage drinking, and she'd shown up looking composed, not a hair out of place. When she'd led him out of there, she hadn't said anything. She'd never laid a hand on him, just given him a look. Worst thing ever.

He knew better than to lie to her. He still did it. "Things are fine."

"You don't sound fine." Luna always knew how he really felt.

"There's nothing actually wrong with me. More like I've got to do something unpleasant."

"Getting mated is a natural thing."

"What? No! That's not it at all." Why would she think that? And why did Poppy come to mind? He grimaced. "If you must know, I'll be embarking shortly on a trip with a few members of the new Feral Pack."

"As part of your investigation on that lead you're following?"

"Yeah. One of them might be able to identify the suspect."

"I assume you're referring to Poppy Smith, formerly Penelope Jameson."

"She's the only witness," he explained.

"Is that the only reason you're bringing her along?"

Rather than lie, he said, "It's not just her. Her brother and two others are coming along too." It soured his mood to even say it out loud.

Laughter emerged from his phone.

"Not funny," he grumbled.

"It is considering how much you enjoy the company of others," she teased.

"I don't hate everyone." Although he came close at times.

"Of course you don't. I'm proud of you for seeking out aid. Finally learning to be a team player."

"It's not the first time," he protested. Why, just recently he'd had another member of the Feral Pack help him shut down bad behavior by an Alpha and his son.

"It's taken you a while, but you're finally learning to trust and maybe even settle down."

The horror of it. "Am not."

"If you say so," Luna sang.

"I don't know why I call you," he grumbled.

"Because if you didn't, I'd worry. If I worried, I'd come after you."

"But not find me. I know how to hide." The familiar banter relaxed him.

"And who taught you that skill?"

His turn to chuckle wryly. "I take it you've been busy while I'm away teaching the next generation?"

"Who, me?" A not-so-innocent lilt.

He reached his hidden SUV and climbed in. "I'll check in once we've reached our destination."

Her tone turned serious. "Be careful, Kit."

"Aren't I always?"

"This time is different. There's something brewing. A disturbance in the world."

"Have you been watching *Star Wars* again?"

"Actually, bingeing Marvel. Delightful story lines, although they could have used some wolves."

He snorted. "Name a movie that wouldn't be better with wolves."

"*The Mitchells vs. The Machines.*"

"Don't you dare say—"

"Dog. Pig. Dog. Pig."

"Loaf of bread," he groaned.

She laughed. "And now you'll be stuck with that in your head."

It would have been if he'd not driven up to the ranch and seen Poppy waiting on the porch.

Then all he could think was, *Woman. Mine. Woman. Mine. Mate.*

Fuck.

EIGHT

Poppy had wondered once Kit left if he'd actually return. He'd been less than impressed with the additions to their party.

Yet he did return, driving a featureless SUV with dark-tinted windows and enough room for three men and a woman, barely. Kit said nothing. Not as they loaded knapsacks and a large cooler in the back. Not as they argued about whose bag should be left behind so they could fit the other bulging fabric cooler she'd packed.

Kit scowled as the whole Pack came to say goodbye, hugging her one at a time with words of encouragement and threats of maiming if she came to harm, Nova's being the most violent: "If anyone harms a hair on your head, I will cut off his dick and make him eat it."

Poppy almost cried.

Rok squeezed her last, lifting her off the ground and growling, "Be careful."

Her reply? "There's a batch of brownies in the freezer hidden under the lasagna."

His eyes widened, and he smiled, a beautiful man all around. There was a time when she'd been infatuated with Rok, his gruff kindness doing much to soothe her, but now that she'd met Kit, the first man to actually pique her interest since her ordeal, she knew why she'd never pursued anything with Rok. She wanted that spark. That loss of breath. That urge to poke his serious ass and see what he'd do. Did Kit have ticklish spots? She kind of wanted to find out.

They piled into the SUV, Kit silent at the wheel, so unlike the three men in the back. They'd all insisted she take the front seat. She wasn't about to argue. She hated getting squished in the middle. This time, Hammer got the joy, his thick shoulders butting into Lochlan on one side and Darian on the other.

She buckled in, and the car moved off. A glance showed Kit's jaw was tense, his gaze flicking often to the rearview mirror and the idiots throwing verbal jabs in the back. Their familiar bickering eased some of her anxiety.

She really should have told one of them to stay home, but they'd been insistent, and how could she choose and not hurt someone's feelings?

Kit's eyes met hers, the blame in his gaze clear.

Such a grumpy enforcer. He needed to learn to loosen up. As Hammer told Lochlan to do something anatomically impossible, she shrugged and grinned.

The poor redheaded enforcer sighed. It made her want to keep count of how many times he'd huff and puff. Three by the time they made their first refueling stop.

Kit had yet to give them an actual destination, just saying it would be about a twenty-seven-hour drive, so a two-day road trip, if all went well.

The first day ended at a motel well after dark, only their third stop of the day since they'd left at dawn. Her ass wasn't happy. As for Kit, he had to be feeling it, given he'd refused to let anyone else drive.

They rented three rooms, each of them in a row with a parking spot in front. Concrete sidewalk, peeling orange-painted doors and windows covered in yellowed venetian blinds. She and Darian got the room in the middle with two beds. Hammer and Lochlan had to share, while Kit got a room to himself. No one offered to bunk with him.

It should be noted that she might have if asked.

She enjoyed his calm and steady presence. It

oddly soothed. Unlike the Pack, he didn't treat her as if she were fragile glass. Which, of course, her brother didn't like.

"He's being rude to you," Darian complained.

"Because he doesn't rush to carry stuff for me?"

"It's called manners," Darian insisted.

"It's called him being aware I'm capable and waiting to be asked. It's actually very respectful."

Darian shot her a look. "You're defending him?"

"Just saying it's nice to be around someone who doesn't act as if I'm some weak ninny who will collapse at the first sign of adversity." The words spewed from her in a rush, and she blinked. Since when did she not need her brother to protect her from all shocks?

The last time was...before her incarceration by Gerard. Used to be, she didn't fear anything, and she never asked for help unless she really needed it.

"I know you're not weak," Darian protested.

"Yet you act as if I am," she replied softly. She felt immediately remorseful. "Ignore me, I'm tired and sore. I'm going to shower before bed." A convenient excuse to leave before she said something that really hurt Darian. If he treated her like she was porcelain, then it was because she'd allowed it. She could have said something instead of leaning on him as hard as she did.

It didn't help that she'd not said no when he'd insisted on coming along. This trip was about facing her past and fears. A past that scared her, because she never wanted to live it again.

She exited the bathroom to see the adjoining door to Lochlan and Hammer's room slightly ajar and Darian's voice coming through the crack. He'd left, giving her space.

Her turn to sigh. Just what was she doing to Darian? She was keeping him from living his own full life and meeting someone, because he played caretaker for her.

Time for that to change. With that thought, she went to bed.

The nightmare hit her hard.

Gerard approached the cage with that sadistic smirk she'd come to hate. He didn't have a needle this time, but the innocuous metal rod in his hand didn't bode well.

"Your healing powers are impressive." He spoke of his experiments on her, where he intentionally caused her harm and then tracked how quickly she healed. "A shame about the scarring, though."

Slashes across her back. Cigarette burns. While she could repair damage to her flesh quicker than a human, she couldn't always rid herself of the evidence after the fact.

"Where's my mother?" Penelope had not seen her since her capture.

"Moaning in bed. She lost the baby." He grimaced. "Should have known better than to use someone her age. My fault. She seemed so healthy. But I have high hopes for you."

Fear hit her. "I won't let you rape me."

"Rape?" He snorted. "You're a bit young for my taste. Besides, I prefer my whores willing and biddable." His view of women disgusted her. How had she and her mother not seen through his fake smiles?

"Why are you doing this?"

"Because I can. And the best part is your kind can't even complain about it, because if you do, the world might find out you exist. And then what?"

"Can't be any worse than what you're doing." He'd been torturing her on and off for a while now. She'd lost track of time. Weeks, months, years. She didn't know, only that it lasted long enough she'd lost hope of being rescued.

"Just carrying on a family tradition."

"Of torture?"

"More like scientific curiosity."

"You're sick," Penelope snapped.

"Not anymore. Your kind has been good for at least one thing." He'd reached the bars with his baton. "Now to see what else you're good for."

Zap.

The electricity hit her, and her teeth clacked together hard enough she bit her tongue and tasted blood. Her whimpering cries didn't stop him from electrocuting her. Even after she hit the floor of her cage and lost control of her bladder, he kept poking at her until she passed out. When she woke, she had new burn marks for him to observe and less hair on her head.

The next time he came at her with the tasing rod, she whimpered. She tried to hold in the screams, but he didn't stop until—

Her shrieks woke Darian, who shook her awake and then hugged her, rocking. "It's okay, Poppy Seed. You're safe."

But for once, she didn't want his comfort. She shoved out of his arms. "I need some air." When Darian would have followed, she shook her head. "Alone, please."

She headed outside to the motel parking lot and glanced up at the sky, which was starting to lighten with dawn. She sensed more than felt Kit approach.

"Sorry I woke you," she muttered.

Kit stood beside her, hands shoved in his pockets. "I used to say the same thing when I woke Luna."

"Luna being...?"

"Foster mom. She rescued me from an abusive

situation when I was young." He didn't add anything more.

She wasn't about to pry, but she did wonder, "When did your nightmares stop?"

"Who says they did?"

"Way to sound encouraging."

"Would you rather I lie?"

She crossed her arms and glared. "Will this mission of yours offer me closure, or was that a lie too?"

"Closure isn't the same as forgetting. If it's any consolation, the intensity and frequency will lessen over time."

Her lips twisted. "How much time? Because it's been years."

"For me, it's been more than thirty, and there are still times I wake up convinced that I'm going to die. Or I'll enter an elevator and feel confined, as if I'm back in a cage."

Her lips parted. "You were kept in a cage too?"

"There are many depraved Gerards in this world."

She turned from him and glanced upward at the sky. "A man who might still be alive. Did it help when you killed the person who hurt you?"

"Wasn't me who did it. Remember, I was just a

child. But the person who saved me ensured he'd never hurt anyone else again."

"I'm sorry."

He appeared startled. "Why?"

"Because hurting people is wrong. Especially a child."

The remark brought a strange quirk to his lips. "While I agree about the children part, I'm not sure about the rest. Sometimes, hurting people is the only way to solve a problem."

Her nose wrinkled. "I forgot for a second you're an enforcer. I guess violence is part of the job."

For some reason, he appeared annoyed. "Not by choice. But keep in mind, when I'm called to duty, it's because someone in a position of power is using it against those who can't defend themselves."

"And you come in to save them as their knight in shining armor?" Her words held a hint of sarcasm.

Laughter barked from him. "I'm hardly the hero type. I creep in with the shadows and handle problematic situations quietly."

"Do you like your job?"

"No. But someone has to do it, and who better than an outcast?"

She eyed him, a man taller than her, with a slim, athletic build. Despite the early hour, he wore a polo shirt and trousers, with loafers slipped on without socks. In the shadows, she couldn't really tell he had red hair, but there was no denying its brightness during the day. There was also no escaping his scent. It circled her now, comforting and at the same time disturbing because it made no sense. Fox. Wolf. And, at times, nothing at all.

"What are you?" she asked.

"I've been called an abomination."

"More like a miracle. You're both fox and wolf. I thought that was impossible." Something about the genetics between the two being incompatible.

Again, he offered a wry smile. "No one knows how I came into existence. The only one of my kind."

"Until you have kids."

His expression turned cold. "I'll never have children."

"You don't like them?"

"On the contrary, they are the only good things in this world. It's more a question of being incapable, which is probably a good thing."

"I wouldn't say that."

"Because you don't know me." A flat statement.

She didn't, and yet, she felt an affinity for this man who might just be as broken inside as she was. It led to her admitting, "I can't have children either."

"I know."

His admission startled her. "How?"

"Your hospital records weren't hard to hack."

It should have occurred to her that since he'd linked her to Gerard, he must have been digging into her past. The reminder of what she'd lost left a sour taste in her mouth. "I used to dream of having a huge family. I had my life planned out. Culinary college then a job working as a sous-chef and getting enough experience to open my own restaurant one day, which I'd leave to my kids when I retired."

"Who says you can't still have that?"

"My lack of womb. The fact I never finished my courses."

"A child doesn't have to be born of your flesh to be family. Colleges are always taking students. And you're already an excellent chef, from what I hear. What's really holding you back is fear."

Astute, even as it burned her that he'd seen through her excuses so easily. "Every day since my escape, I've been waiting for Gerard to find me. To finish what he started."

"Do you want to die?"

At the odd question, she snorted. "No."

"Then stop letting him live rent-free in your head and start living."

"I want to."

"Then do it."

"It's not that simple."

"I know it's not. Life is hard. Harder for some than others. But you're not a coward."

"Aren't I?" She'd been hiding from the world.

"Some people would kill themselves rather than face living after trauma."

"There are days I still think about doing it." A hard admission to make, and one she'd never told anyone else.

"When those moments happen, remember you're not alone." With those words, he reached for her hand and clasped it.

Kept holding it as the dawn crested the horizon.

And for the first time in a long time, she wasn't afraid.

NINE

Sappy. He was a sappy fucking idiot. Kit chastised himself as he showered and readied for their departure.

His own fault. He'd known even before she woke screaming that she suffered. Despite doing his best to ignore her, he'd managed to achieve a strange affinity for her. He knew where she was pretty much at all times. Could sense her moods.

When he'd heard the door to the room beside his open, he'd been watching from the window. He couldn't bear to see her outside alone. Hugging herself. Sad. Afraid.

The conversation between them had revealed more than he'd intended, but he'd been unable to help himself. Poppy needed to know she wasn't alone. That there were some who understood.

But that didn't explain why he'd held her fucking hand while watching the fucking sunrise.

Worse, he'd never felt so content.

It had led to him being brusque when he'd abruptly said, "Tell your brother and friends we leave in thirty minutes."

Which was more like an hour, since they insisted on a proper breakfast. Apparently, a protein shake wasn't a meal. Neither was the greasy food they insisted on from the tiny restaurant on-site.

Then another day in Hell proceeded in which the only bright spot was Poppy in the front seat beside him, turning a few shy smiles in his direction and rolling her eyes when the men in the back began complaining about who farted.

It was Hammer. Probably because of that damned breakfast.

When his SUV broke down, though, Kit blamed them all. He glared at the steaming engine of the SUV, parked on the side of the highway, its hood open. He'd paid cash for it and put some bogus plates on it. At a few years old, it shouldn't have had an issue.

All of them eyed the inner workings as if they had a fucking clue or the right tools. They didn't. Nor could they get a signal in this cell-forsaken place. Kit glared at the zero bars on his phone and wished he'd pushed harder for a proper satellite phone, but those were expensive and more traceable than a throwaway bought with cash at a store.

With few options, Lochlan and Hammer began walking to find them some help, leaving Kit alone with Poppy and her brother.

Kit would have preferred to be anywhere else, because Darian glared. A lot. The reason became clear when Poppy left for some privacy in the woods.

Darian barely waited for her to get out of earshot before threatening, "Stay away from my sister."

"Kind of hard, given the car lacks the room to social distance," was his smartass retort.

"I've seen the way you're eyeing her. She's not for the likes of you."

Kit actually agreed. However, in the spirit of being ornery, he stated, "That's not really up to you."

"Fucking right it is. She's my baby sister."

"She's a grown woman being smothered by a well-meaning family." The words emerged harsher than he'd intended, and Darian sucked in a breath.

"It's not smothering, you cold bastard. It's called caring."

"If you cared, you'd have done something about her nightmares a long time ago."

"She won't see a shrink. And even if she did, it isn't as if she can tell one what really happened."

"So instead, you let her fester in her fear."

"As opposed to what? What else could I do? I tried to kill the bastard. I thought when he went into the house and didn't come back out that he burned with it."

"Did you ever try to find out for sure?"

"No." A sulky reply. "I had to take care of Poppy."

"Speaking of which, you could have installed security cameras for her peace of mind. I can't believe how easy it was to spy on your Pack."

"I told Rok we should get some," Darian grumbled.

"You could have signed her up for self-defense classes."

"Poppy's not a fighter."

"Bullshit. She's fighting every day to get out of bed and not let the fear win. How did it not occur to you that knowing how to protect herself might help?" Kit could see Darian's expression falling, but he kept hammering. "You could have done things to show her she can still have the life she wanted. Enrolled her in culinary classes. Stayed in a city so she could work as a cook."

"She cooks for us at the ranch!" Darian hotly defended.

"It's not the same, and you know it."

"What makes you the fucking expert?" Darian snapped.

"My job is dealing with the aftermath of those who are abused."

"Meaning you kill the perpetrator."

"If the crime merits it, then yes. But I'm also the one ensuring the victims are taken care of."

"Oh, really? Where were you when my sister was being tortured? When that fucker kept her in a cage and used her as his punching bag? When he whipped her? And burned her?"

Each accusation hit Kit hard, but at the same time, he knew better than to accept the blame. "At the time, I was in France hunting down a feral. I didn't know about the trouble. But you should have. Or are you going to tell me you didn't notice the fact your mom and sister stopped communicating with you?"

"I was overseas on a mission. I never even knew until I returned to base and I got a garbled message from my mom." Darian rubbed a hand over his face. "I asked for leave, and it was granted, but by the time I arrived, I was too late."

"And yet, you expected the Lykosium to magically be aware?" Kit replied softly. "We do our best, but we aren't omniscient."

Darian sighed and leaned against the broken-down car. "I know, but it's easier to blame you."

"How about we blame the true villain instead?"

Darian grimace. "To this day, I still don't know how Gerard knew about us. Poppy swears she never saw him when she shifted. And Mom rarely went out as a wolf."

Kit's turn to roll his shoulders. "No idea, but if this guy we're checking out turns out to be that asshole, maybe we'll find out."

"And then we'll kill him."

"We'll take him into custody," Kit corrected.

Darian shoved off the vehicle. "Wait, you're taking him alive?"

"Only so he can be questioned. We need to know if our secret's been compromised. And if yes, we need to know the extent it's been compromised so we can do damage control."

At Darian's glance at the woods, Kit added, "I promise, once we've gotten everything we need, he will die. Slowly and painfully."

At that, Darian nodded. "Fine. But do me a favor. Don't tell Poppy."

"Tell Poppy what?" she declared, coming out of the bush. "I'm not a child, Darian. And I heard everything." While her brother blushed, Kit remained stony-faced.

Until she eyed him and said, "What if I want to

ask Gerard some questions?"

"We don't know it's him."

She rolled her eyes. "I know. I'm talking about if he is."

"Then you'll get your chance." Because she deserved an opportunity to find closure.

"What if I want to be the one who ends his life?"

Some would say no, to prevent further trauma. As a victim himself, though, Kit sometimes wished Luna had left his abusers alive so he could have been the one to end them.

His lips flattened. "You wanna hurt or kill him, then I'll loan you whatever weapon you want."

"As if I need one," her dry retort.

As for Darian... "Poppy!"

As the siblings started to bicker, Kit wandered off, disturbed that Darian thought him interested in Poppy. He'd been trying so hard to avoid her, and then he'd talked to her, shared, held her hand.

Ugh. He'd have to keep his distance from now on.

The SUV eventually got towed, and they learned repairs would take a few days, given a part had to be ordered for the radiator.

Kit couldn't wait that long. The quicker he completed his mission, the faster he went home and left Penelope behind.

"How can I get to the city?" he asked the mechanic. The small hamlet didn't have a used-car dealership, or a bus, or a train. Just an old truck for sale, the kind with only a front bench seat.

That led to a major argument among the men that Darian, of course, won. Lochlan and Hammer would remain behind and follow when the repairs on the SUV were done.

Since Kit hated driving a clutch, he finally let Darian have a turn at the wheel. With Penelope sitting between them in the old truck that smelled of dog—a golden retriever, judging by the hair—they set off.

And Kit was more aware than ever of the woman beside him.

The delay on the road meant one more night in a motel. But rather than Penelope sharing a room with her brother, Darian slung an arm around Kit's shoulders and said to his sister, "You take the second bedroom. I'll bunk with our enforcer."

Only once the door was closed did Kit growl, "What the fuck? We're not sharing. I'll rent another room."

"I'm not going to be sleeping here. I need to blow off some steam."

Kit caught on quickly. "Okay. Sure."

"I'll leave the door between the rooms open a

crack in case anything happens. I'll be back before dawn."

"What if she asks where you are?" Kit eyed the door between the rooms. They'd be alone together, but separated. No problem.

"Tell her I'm out having a few beers." Darian wagged a finger. "No hanky-fucking-panky or, Lykosium or not, I will beat your ass until it matches your hair."

"Go ahead and try," was Kit's dry reply.

"Don't threaten him!" Penelope entered the room and shook a finger at Darian.

"Fuck me, he doesn't need you protecting him," Darian argued, stalking to loom over her.

She met him glare for glare. "I don't need you butting into my affairs."

"Don't you dare get involved with him."

"I will do what I like with who I like," was her sassy reply.

"Over my dead body."

"Tell you what, if you're so worried about my virtue, then how about you treat the next woman you meet at a bar how you'd like to see me treated."

Darian's pained expression had Kit laughing.

"Poppy, you're being unreasonable. I'm just looking out for you."

"I can look after myself," she stated, still

scowling.

"Maybe I should stay." Darian eyed the door then his sister.

"Go have a few beers. I'll be fine." She shoved her brother out the door then turned on Kit with a roll of her eyes. "He's worse than a mother hen sometimes."

"Because he loves you."

"A little too much sometimes. Is your adopted mom like that?"

"Luna is more about shoving me at anyone in hopes I'll settle down."

"Haven't found the right person yet?" she quipped.

He had to glance away to lie. "Nope."

"Oh. Me either," she said on a high note. "Guess I'll go watch some television."

He almost invited her to stay with him.

Instead, he said not a word as she left the room and went next door. He lay on the bed, his own television off, arm under his head, all too aware she remained literally a few paces away.

Getting involved? Bad idea, even as he had a harder and harder time figuring out just why they shouldn't.

The question chased him into sleep, where he remembered why he shouldn't care.

TEN

POPPY AWOKE IN DARKNESS LIT ONLY BY A STRIP of neon that sliced through the top of the curtains.

She listened—and hoped she'd imagined it. Only, she'd have sworn she heard movement. Her head turned toward the door between the rooms. Kit was on the other side. Darian, too, if he'd returned from his bar hopping—code-speak for *getting laid*. As if she didn't know.

Nothing broke the quiet. Still, she rose from bed, wearing shorts and a tank top, and headed for the door to peek through. The same neon light came through the gap between the curtains, enough for her to see only one bed occupied.

Kit.

A restless Kit whose limbs spasmed, his arms

flinging out, his legs twitching. His head turned from side to side. He shuddered.

He wore only boxers, his upper body bare, and tense. Muscled too. He had scars, most of them the silvery white of age, the ridged marks telling a story she wanted to hear.

On silent feet, she approached the side of the bed, sensing his agitation. His panic.

He dreamed. Not a pleasant one. She couldn't help herself and reached out to touch him.

And fell into his dream.

She found herself in a clearing, standing on four furry legs as a small red shape emerged from the woods. Not alone. Another red fox appeared, then a third one, all trying to bolt for the far side.

But the safety they sought was blocked by men on horses, brandishing spears that they jabbed at the small foxes. They paused in the center of the field, hemmed in by pointed spears on one side, a line of slavering dogs on the other.

The foxes seemed screwed, but then a furry shape landed in the clearing, a large fox that was more golden than red, her tail a sinuous thing that pushed the little foxes back as she handled the first dog.

The savage battle didn't last long. The canines fled before the female turned on the hunters with a growl, once more tucking her kits behind her.

The men didn't have any consideration for the mother. She fought valiantly, maimed two of the humans, but in the end, she died. And the little foxes wailed.

She didn't realize she gasped for air until Kit shook her. "Wake up."

She blinked at him. "I saw...I—"

"Nothing. You had a bad dream."

"But the hunters... The fox..."

His eyes blazed. "I didn't say you could look inside my head."

Was that what she'd done? "I didn't mean to. I saw you having a nightmare and simply tried to wake you. I'm sorry." Her chin dropped. She closed her eyes, trying to forget the violence she'd seen. Then she realized she was sitting in his lap.

He sighed. "I'm the one who's sorry. I shouldn't have been a dick."

"You weren't lying when you said you still have nightmares."

He shrugged. "Every so often, one will hit. I wake up. It's done. No big deal."

"I can't wait to get to that point." She leaned her head against his chest, soothed by the steady thump of his heart.

"It will happen."

"Promise?" she teased.

To her surprise, he replied, "Promise. Now, you should go back to your bed."

"I'm comfortable, though." She remained lying against him.

"This isn't appropriate."

She snorted. "According to who?"

"Your brother, for one."

"Darian won't be back before dawn unless he strikes out. Which has never happened, from my understanding."

"You're close to your brother."

"Too close at times. He's always been protective, but it went up a few notches after my ordeal." She turned to rub her face against Kit's chest.

"Does it bother you?"

"It didn't used to. At the time, I needed to feel protected."

"Not anymore?"

"I don't know. I thought I did. I never realized how confining it felt until you came along."

His chest shook as he chuckled. "Ever notice how we sometimes build our own cages?"

"What kind of cage do you keep yourself in?"

At first, he said nothing but, then, muttered in a low tone, "I don't like people to get close to me."

Her cheek against his flesh, she whispered, "You're not pushing me away."

"I'm aware."

She tilted her head to see his face. "Why? Afraid I'll break?"

He barked a short laugh. "My reasons are more selfish."

She squirmed on his lap, his erection evident. "And will you act on those reasons?"

"No." He spoke firmly, yet he didn't remove her.

She nipped the edge of his chin. "What if I wanted you to?"

"I'd remind you this is the wrong time and place."

"When is the right time and where?"

"Never and nowhere, because this can't happen."

"Why?"

"I'm not playing this game, Penelope."

Her nose scrunched. "I haven't heard that in a long time. Everyone calls me Poppy."

"A delicate flower. I'm surprised you allow it."

"What should I be called? And don't say Penelope. I stopped being her after Gerard."

"Something fierce, like you. Strong and loyal."

"Like a vixen protecting her babies." She regretted reminding him as he stiffened. When he would have set her off his lap, she wound her arms around his neck.

"Why is it, with you, I don't feel broken?" she asked, forcing his gaze to meet hers.

"Because compared to me, you're perfect."

"Says the beautiful man," she murmured.

"Said no woman ever of a redheaded devil." His crooked smile held a self-deprecating note.

"Aren't we a pair? Both of us convinced we're not good enough for anyone. Maybe that's why I know you're my mate."

ELEVEN

Kᴛ ꜰʀᴏᴢᴇ ᴀꜱ ꜱʜᴇ ꜱᴀɪᴅ ɪᴛ.

You're my mate.

For some reason, he'd not thought her affected by the same need burning inside him. After all, she treated him no differently than anyone else. Except for the fact she was sitting in his lap, pressed against him, putting pressure on a part of him that would have liked less clothes.

"Did you forget how to speak?" she teased, but he could hear the nervousness underneath the tone. As if she feared she'd revealed too much.

He could have assuaged that anxiety by saying, *Yes, you're my fucking mate.* And then taken her in a passionate blaze of glory.

But Kit being Kit, he just couldn't be like everyone else who met their mate.

He stood, a firm grip making her rise with him. When he knew she stood on her own two feet, he released her.

"What you're feeling is a passing infatuation for someone who isn't like a brother to you. It will pass."

She cocked her head, but rather than look hurt by his rejection, a smile ghosted her lips. "I can promise I don't think of you as my brother. For one, I never kissed my brother like this." She moved faster than he could react.

Or was it he didn't want to move out of the way of her lips, which latched suddenly onto his?

She kissed him, the heat simmering within unfurling into a rush of molten desire. For a second, he kissed her back, his hands palming her ass and tugging her closer.

It was fucking glorious.

She made a noise, a needy grumble. It would be so easy to satisfy their urges. But then what? What happened after the passion cooled and she had regrets the next day?

He set her aside. "We shouldn't do this."

"I disagree. However, if that's how you feel. Good night, my sexy fox."

My?

He stood stunned as she left him with a swing to her hips, a come-hither peek over her shoulder and, as she stepped into the other room, a softly chuckled, "You know where to find me. I'll be waiting."

Fuck waiting. He took a step in her direction, only to pause and swing his head around at a noise. It took him only three strides to reach the door and fling it open.

In stumbled Darian, face bloody, one eye swollen shut.

"What happened to you?" Kit grunted as the man went partially limp and he had to support all of Darian's weight.

"Tried to play the good guy. Got beaten for my trouble," Darian slurred.

"This better not be a fight over a girl again."

Penelope, like a penny, returned.

"Sorry I woke you." Darian tried to sit up, but Kit shoved him back down.

"Don't move. Let's check you over for broken bones." Because they'd have to be set before they started fusing back together, a quicker process for most Were.

"Bones are fine. They were mostly about softening me up to rob me. They didn't get my wallet," Darian added with a bloody grin.

"Because they could have done so much with your pay-as-you-go credit card and twenty bucks in cash," his sister said.

"It's the point of it," Darian argued.

Kit understood. "Never let bottom-feeders think they can get away with it. The more people say no to bad behaviors and give them consequences, the less likely they'll do it."

"Or you could hand it over, avoid a beating, and buy another wallet," she pointed out.

"Must be nice to have that privilege," Kit drawled.

"As if you weren't raised with wealth," Darian chimed in. "I know who your mom is. She is high up in the Lykosium."

His Penny—who he'd yet to decide was lucky or not—eyed him. "She's the Luna I heard of on the council. Meadow told us about her. I should have made the connection before."

"I don't advertise our relationship because it's not important." Kit had done things the hard way to avoid people accusing him of using Luna's position to help himself.

"You said before she saved you. Did she used to be an enforcer?"

He snorted. "The best, as she likes to remind me. Can't disagree, given she arrived in time to save me."

"Whereas I was too late," a drunk Darian lamented.

Penny placed her hand on her brother's arm.

"What happened wasn't your fault. There were things I could have done. That Mom could have."

"Don't you dare play the coulda, shoulda, woulda game," Kit exclaimed in a firm tone. "Shit happens. Bad shit. We deal with it and move on."

"Says the guy who won't," Penny muttered.

He offered her a side-eye. He wanted to ask her what she meant, but Darian watched and listened a little too intently. He also noticed things. "You came awfully quick, sis. Were you awake? Did you have a bad dream?"

"I did." Kit jumped in to spare her the brotherly concern.

"You?" Darian's lip curled.

She jumped to his rescue. "Be nice. He's gone through more than you could ever understand."

As if a glaring Darian cared. "If I didn't know better, I'd think you have the hots for the enforcer."

"Why shouldn't I? He's handsome." Her chin went up, as if she defied him to say otherwise.

"I have questions about your taste," was Darian's sour reply.

To which Kit couldn't help but quip, "I'd say it's excellent."

"Stay out of it," Darian grumbled.

"No, you stay out of it," Penny chided. "If I want

to have a relationship with Kit, I will, and I don't care if either of you don't like it."

With that declaration, she stalked off, leaving both Darian and Kit staring.

The silence broke when Darian huffed, "Why don't you want to date my sister?"

TWELVE

THE NEXT DAY, KIT WOULDN'T MEET HER EYES. Her brother, on the other hand, did everything he could to shove Poppy at Kit. She didn't understand the sudden shift in his mood. So on their last stop before their final destination, she yanked Darian aside. "Okay. Spill it. Why are you trying to rub me in Kit's face?"

"It's obvious you like the boy. And it occurs to me that this is the first crush you've had since Rok."

"I did not crush on Rok," she huffed, embarrassed that it might have been obvious.

"Whatever." Darian waved off her lie. "Here I've been forbidding him from going near you, when he's actually perfect for you to get back on the dating horse." He beamed as he said it, only to then frown.

"Not that you should be doing any riding...er, or, that is..." He stopped stammering and turned red.

"I am not a virgin, Darian." She just hadn't had sex since she'd left college. How many years of doing nothing would it take before she became an honorary virgin?

"I know. I don't... I mean, I don't care. Don't tell me." He started to pace. "What I'm saying is, if you want to flirt and date the fox, then go ahead. I won't be a dick about it, because I should be encouraging you to get out there."

"How about I do what I want and you just support me?"

"I will not support another foray into veganism." He shook his finger.

A short-lived fad. She grinned. "Fair enough."

They shook on it.

As Kit arrived, he eyed them suspiciously. "Why do you both appear smug?"

Now that she knew Darian wouldn't get in the way, and with her own anxiety finally taking a step back, she was determined to feel alive again with the man scowling at her.

She linked her arm with his. "Just saying it's been a long trip, but we're finally here. One step closer to getting closure."

That didn't smooth his brow. "*If* this man is Gerard."

"Even if he's not, if someone is hurting Were, I want to help stop them. Maybe being part of the solution against violence will also provide closure. After all, it worked for you."

"What makes you say that?"

"Isn't that why you became an enforcer?"

With that, she winked and slid into the back seat for once, forcing her brother into the front with Kit. A man who kept glancing at her in the rearview.

A man in need of seduction tonight, before the danger they'd encounter tomorrow.

Rather than a hotel for their stay, he'd rented a house a few blocks from their target. She eyed the two-story suburban place and said, "It's a nice place to raise kids."

"Needs more yard space," was Kit's comment as he opened the combination lock and withdrew the key.

"How would you know what a kid needs?" Darian's reply was snarky as he stalked inside.

"Ignore him."

"Already am," Kit riposted with a half-grin. "Place is three bedrooms, but one has been converted into a home gym. You take the master. Your brother can have the spare."

"What about you?"

"Couch will be fine."

She eyed the couch that was not long enough for his frame. With Darian out of sight, she leaned close and whispered, "Or you could join me?" She planted the seed and sauntered off to find the kitchen. The slam of the door didn't surprise her.

When Kit returned a few hours later, it was to find her cooking in the kitchen, the one place she always felt at ease. This time, she was determined to see if she could wiggle her way into a man's heart with good food.

"Dinner's almost ready," she sang.

"How?" Kit glanced at the array of dishes being prepared. "I didn't think the place came with food."

"It didn't. I hit a grocery store."

He blinked at her. "You went out."

"There's a lovely market about a fifteen-minute walk away."

"You shouldn't have done that."

She closed the oven. "Why not?"

His mouth opened and closed. "Because we're supposed to be under cover."

"I highly doubt our rich target is shopping for himself at a local store."

He scowled. "Still. What if he saw you?"

"I thought the whole point was for me to confirm that Gerard is here."

"Not alone!"

"Calm down. Nothing happened," she soothed. "Sit. Dinner is about to be served." She pointed to the table.

He slid into a seat. "Where's your brother?"

"Jogging."

"During dinner?"

"He wanted to eyeball the place in daylight. So his plan was to jog past it and then stop somewhere to eat. He'll come back when it's dark so he can see it after hours."

"Is he trying to get caught?"

"He looks nothing like the military grunt Gerard met before. Why do you think he's been growing out the facial hair the last few days?"

She placed a steaming plate in front of him. A breaded chicken breast sat atop pasta in a creamy sauce sprinkled with chunks of bacon, all covered with a light layer of parmesan petals.

He eyed it. "You made this?"

She nodded. "My version of creamy chicken carbonara with caramelized onions, mushrooms, and sauteed asparagus."

He actually groaned as he ate it.

She'd never been happier to feed someone.

When he finished, he eyed her with an expression that warmed her right to her toes.

"That was delicious."

"I'm glad you liked it. Do you have room for dessert?"

He glanced at his belly. "Fuck it. I'll probably regret it if I say no."

He definitely would have. From the fridge, she removed tiramisu made with layers of strawberries, cake, and whipped cream.

She set the bowl in front of him with a single spoon.

"Aren't you having any?" he asked.

"It's best when shared." She plopped herself onto his lap, which took a bit of wedging, given his chair was only partially turned from the table.

He stilled. "What are you doing?"

"Having dessert." She spooned up some tiramisu and popped it into her mouth. "Mmm." The next ladle went to his lips.

He hesitated before opening and then groaned again. "Are you sure I have to share?"

That brought a giggle to her lips. "Yes."

The next scoop went to her mouth and smeared her lips. She leaned forward, and he didn't say a word, just licked off the cream, and then he kissed her. The sweetness of the dessert was not needed, because the taste of him was all she craved. All she wanted.

The chair made a little noise as he shoved it back enough so she could turn to straddle him. She cupped his jaw while she kissed him, and his hands palmed her ass. Every slide of lips, lick of a tongue, grind of her pelvis had her breath hitching.

Her desire pulsed with want for the first time in forever. She made little noises as she rocked on him, the pressure of his erection giving her the friction she wanted. It had been so long.

She had a mini orgasm on his lap and cried out into his mouth. His arms tightened around her, and he shuddered.

"Fuck me, Penny, what are you doing to me?" A shaky query.

"Trying to get you to seduce me," was her soft reply as she kept kissing him.

He stood abruptly, keeping her in his arms. Her legs wrapped around his waist.

She had no doubt they'd end up in bed. Wanted it.

The door to the house slammed open as Darian returned early, exclaiming, "I think I saw Mom."

THIRTEEN

As cold showers went, Darian's arrival and statement shocked the arousal right out of Kit. Poor Penny groaned and muttered, "His timing is shit."

As she unwrapped herself from him and busied herself at the sink, Kit had just enough time to sit down and hide the slowly fading erection before Darian stalked into the kitchen, wild-eyed.

"Did you hear me? I said I saw Mom!" Darian reiterated.

Penny turned from the counter, wiping her hands on a towel. "I heard you sounding crazy. Mom is dead. We both saw her body. Buried her."

"I know. It's fucking nuts, but as I was jogging by that house, I saw her in the backseat of a car coming out. And she looked just fucking like Mom. Hair, build, face." Darian gestured with his hands, while Kit accessed a file on his phone. He pulled up an image.

"Was this the woman?"

Darian snatched the phone and exclaimed, "Yes. Fuck. Is it her?" He thrust it at Penny, who took it with obvious reluctance.

At first, her expression showed shock, but the longer she looked, the more her brow creased. She shook her head. "Similar, but it's not her. This woman has a mole on her left cheekbone, and Mom's eyes were not that shade."

"Interesting that you think there's that great of a resemblance," Kit remarked, taking back his phone. "We got this image from Kline's social media. Far as we can tell, she lives with Kline. We're assuming she's Kline's girlfriend."

Darian grimaced. "If this Theodore is actually Gerard, then it's kind of sick he's dating a Mom look-alike."

"Is she Were?" Penny aimed her astute query at Kit.

He shrugged. "No idea. We don't have a name to run, and I haven't gotten close enough yet to find out." He eyed Darian. "Did you scent her?"

"No. The car windows were shut." Darian's lips

turned down. "Won't him having a girlfriend make it harder for Poppy to get inside?" He flopped into a chair and dragged the dessert over.

A dessert that had tasted sweeter when eaten off Penny's lips and tongue.

Kit looked away. Now was not the time to be remembering how she'd embraced him. She'd made it clear she wanted him. He'd have taken her, too, if not for the interruption.

"If it's Gerard, I don't think he'll ignore an opportunity to get his hands on me again." Kit caught the tremble of her hands as she filled the dishwasher. He didn't offer to help, because he knew she needed the distraction. For all her bravery, the prospect of seeing her abuser face-to-face terrified her.

"If it's him," Kit reiterated. "Which reminds me, I have to get something." He left the room and returned with a small locked case. He set it on the table while Darian continued to shovel dessert into his mouth.

"What is that?" Penny asked, folding the towel over the handle on the oven door before nearing. If Darian hadn't been sitting there, he would have dragged her into his lap and kissed her until that concerned look disappeared from her eyes.

Instead, he dialed the combination and flipped

open the lid. A few cartridges and a syringe sat within. "Each of these tubes contains a micro tracking chip."

Darian paused. "You are not chipping my sister like a dog."

"How good of a range does it have?" she asked, ignoring her brother.

"It works by bouncing a signal off cell phone towers, so pretty good."

"So long as she stays inside the city," Darian pointed out.

"Most of the country has coverage now."

"Most, not all," Darian argued. "We all know there's areas where the signal gets skewed and dropped."

Penny sighed. "Would you rather I get kidnapped and not found at all?"

Her brother's jaw dropped. "'Course not."

"Then shut up, because I'm getting one, and so are you."

"Me?" Darian sounded surprised.

"You forget, Gerard didn't imprison me because I'm a girl. He's just as likely to cage you. And I can't lose you."

Darian's shoulders slumped. "Fine."

Kit cleared his throat. "If it makes you feel better, I have three in my body now. Luna injects me with a new one the moment she thinks the old one isn't working." She was overprotective in some respects, but at the same time, she always encouraged him to go out and act.

"Do it." Penny held out her arm.

He injected it under her skin, the chip virtually undetectable. Only thickly insulated walls or an EMP pulse could disrupt the signal.

"Will I get better Wi-Fi reception now?" Penny joked.

"Move to Europe, and you will." The words slipped from his lips, and he could have smacked himself.

Darian didn't notice, but she did. Her glance at him held a smile. "Always wanted to see more of the world."

What did that mean?

"Who's spying on the place tonight?" Darian asked after he got his microchip.

"Not you. You've already jogged past. If they see you again, they'll get suspicious." Kit tried to focus on the task and not the distracting woman. "The neighborhood isn't so developed that a fox would be out of place."

"From what I've heard, you're bigger than a normal fox," the cockblocker pointed out.

"Most people won't know that," Kit argued.

"Why even watch the house at night? Are you expecting something to happen?" Penny slid into the empty seat between Kit and Darian.

"It would be good to know what to expect. Comings and goings. Times where there's more activity. Night patrols."

"What if you and I took a walk together?" she suggested. "A couple enjoying the evening air, stopping every so often to canoodle."

"Er..." Kit had no reply because he'd never canoodled. But now that she'd suggested it, he totally wanted to.

Darian grimaced. "Gross, but it would work because people don't pay attention to couples making out."

"Aren't you going to threaten to punch me if I do?" Kit hadn't forgotten the earlier warnings.

At the reminder, Darian shrugged. "Poppy's a grown woman. She knows how to say no and knee you in the balls if you push her too far."

Said balls tightened.

"It's a plan, then. Ready, my hot fox of a boyfriend?" She winked.

He almost groaned. He definitely hardened. And when they went outside, exposed to all threats, he understood at last why everyone hovered around

Penny. He wanted to spirit her away from this place to somewhere safe.

I can't let anything happen to her.

Because he'd finally found the one thing he couldn't be cold and objective about.

FOURTEEN

K it walked stiffly at Poppy's side, her arm looped through his, the only thing shortening his strides.

"We're supposed to be a couple in love," she reminded as they neared the address of interest.

He halted entirely. "I've never been in love."

The admission startled. "Ever? Surely you've dated." He was too handsome not to be chased by women.

"Yeah, I've dated, but nothing really serious." He rolled his shoulders. "Never found anyone I connected with."

She could have sworn she heard him say *until now*, but his lips had stopped moving.

She squeezed his arm. "I thought I was once, in high school. But he turned out to be a jerk."

"Then it wasn't really love."

"I guess not. Do you want to find someone?" she asked, trying to not look too eager to hear his answer.

"Never thought about it, quite honestly. My life isn't exactly conducive to being in a relationship. I travel extensively."

"And?"

"No one wants to spend most of their time home alone," he retorted.

"Did it ever occur to you to find a partner? Someone who could travel with you?"

"No."

A solid refusal, and yet, she refused to give up. "I've always wanted to experience more of the world. Taste new cuisine. Immerse myself in local flavors."

"Then do it."

"You make it sound easy," she said with a laugh as they resumed walking.

"Because it is. And before you give me excuses, let's be honest—if Gerard wanted to find you, he could."

"We changed our last name."

"To the most common one in the world." He snorted. "All it would take is him running a facial-recognition scan on some databases with driver's licenses and he'd have found you."

"Is that how you found our suspect?"

He shook his head. "The few images I dug up look nothing like this guy. It's the similarities of events that led me to him. Not to mention the last name."

"What if he's not Gerard?"

"Then whoever he is will still require investigation, because if they are hunting down Were, then they have to be stopped."

"You're sounding like a hero again."

He grimaced. "Fuck that."

She turned on him suddenly and cupped his cheeks. "Don't be so hard on yourself." She leaned up and kissed him before whispering, "We shouldn't be arguing. We're in sight of the property."

He groaned into her mouth. "Why must you be so distracting?"

A soft laugh escaped her. "Only to you, my sexy fox." She embraced him once more, just because she wanted to, before they resumed walking. She tried to not tense when she saw the stone wall surrounding the property. It was topped with spikes, and electrified, according to Kit, making the property difficult to enter on the sly.

Before the main gate, which had an electronic pad and monitor, he swung her into his arms, nuzzling her ear and muttering, "Cameras are watching and listening."

Who cared? His mouth interested her more, as did the hands roaming her back.

A sharp whistle and a shouted, "Hey, take that shit elsewhere," brought her back to the moment.

Her cheeks blazed as she turned to see a scowling security guard behind the gate.

Kit offered a smooth smile. "Sorry if two people in love bothers you."

"Be in love somewhere else."

Kit glanced down at the sidewalk then back to the man. "You don't get to tell me what to do on public property."

"Listen, you fucking ginger—"

"Darling, don't start a fight. It's not worth it. Besides, I'd rather be somewhere private with you." She batted her lashes at Kit and then offered a conciliatory smile to the guy. "Sorry. He's been away on business, and we're still catching up."

The guard didn't soften one bit, nor did his hand move from his holster. Poppy remained all too aware that the video cameras caught a full view of her face.

If Gerard watched, he'd know her. Her hair might be longer, her features somewhat matured, but she'd be recognizable.

"Git, before I call the cops and report you for indecent acts on public property." The guard wouldn't budge.

Arm in arm, they strolled on, Kit tense and angry. As they passed out of sight of the guard and cameras, she tugged him to a stop in front of the next home, surrounded by only a wrought-iron fence, put her arms around his neck, and whispered, "Calm, my fox."

"I don't like the way he talked to you," Kit growled.

"He was just as rude to you." She cupped his cheek. "And we learned a lot. We now know someone is guarding the gate and he's armed."

He took a breath and let it out. "He had a gun, a Taser, a knife, and zip ties. There was also a walkie attached to his belt."

"Seems like overkill to me. This is a nice neighborhood." Each house was on an acre lot. If one ignored the larger size of the home they were watching and its excessive security, it had a very suburban feel to it. Especially dropped as it was in the middle of a block and surrounded by other mini mansions.

"It's a rich area that people want to protect."

She waved a hand at the property behind them. "That usually means putting up a fence, maybe a few cameras, not having some wannabe mercenary at the gate. Only people with something to hide do that."

"Only one way to find out. I need a way inside."

She shuffled back to the fence, dragging him with her, lifting her lips to his and sliding him a kiss and a whispered, "The neighbors' place isn't as well guarded."

"They're also home," he observed, a hand threading through her hair, cradling her head.

"Will they notice if they have some furry visitors?"

"It's too dangerous." He pulled back slightly, and she grabbed him to yank him back to her mouth.

"Aren't you the one who keeps telling me to stop hiding?"

He groaned. "From life, not bad guys."

"Possible bad guys." She nipped his lower lip. "And besides, I have an idea."

FIFTEEN

Penny's idea was bad. But only because it involved her. In reality, she'd made a great suggestion.

The fence around Kline's neighbors' house proved easy to climb, given the tree branch extending over the sidewalk. Even better, there were no cameras watching. Once in the yard, Penny held his hand as they threaded through the shrubbery and past the house. Only a few windows were lit, the main one in the front showing the flickering of a screen as someone watched television.

They snuck past, Penny grinning as if this were some teenage prank. It was harder than it should be to not join her, because he did feel lighter and happier.

The pool in the back wasn't covered, and the

lights were off. In the shadows, they made their way to the pool cabana, the structure set about a meter back from the fence.

He cupped his hands to give her a boost onto the cabana roof. She crouched and waited for him to join her. He didn't need to touch the spikes topping the section of wall before them to feel the electricity coursing through them. Cameras also existed on this side, but they weren't pointed at the neighboring yard because, as she'd remarked when she'd whispered her plan, *No one wants to be spied on in their pool or hot tub.* Especially since most people liked to use the latter while naked.

No cameras aimed this way meant they could observe the house next door without trouble. Unlike the yard they hid in, the one next door had a fully lit pool, the underwater lights changing every so often. The patio itself had strings of small LEDs wrapped around the overhang and down the columns supporting it. The sliding door had its curtain pulled, as did all the windows, with only a few showing cracks of light.

Poppy stood on the cabana roof, and before he could ask what she was thinking, she vaulted over the fence.

He blinked. He'd forgotten she'd done gymnastics in high school. She hit the other side and immediately crouched. She glanced at him, her gaze saying, *Your turn.*

Kit might be able to do many things, but flipping and landing without breaking something wasn't one of them. That didn't stop him. He wouldn't leave her alone in enemy territory.

He did a quick strip before shifting into his fox. He leaped across the fence, hoping he wouldn't snap a leg. He hit, not gracefully, and smacked his snout in the grass, which was soft at least.

A hand stroked down his back as his lucky Penny leaned close to whisper, "There's my handsome fox."

He uttered a snort. Never mind that Luna called him the same thing. He knew he was a mishmash of parts. Only his coloring was predominantly fox.

Penny put a finger to her lips and pointed left.

He'd already heard the approaching steps. Of more concern: The moment they strayed from this wall and the bush they'd landed beside, the cameras would catch any motion. Penny hugged the wall and sidled to the tree where the motion detector was strapped, keeping out of range of sight. She ducked under the motion detector and kept moving sideways, having an uncanny second sense for where to move to avoid being seen.

To a man like Kit, used to moving in shadows, it proved to be extremely sexy. They made it to the outer part of the patio, where junglelike foliage provide privacy from the neighbors and a place for them to hide and peek.

She leaned close and in a hushed voice said, "I can't see anything from here. I'm going to get closer."

He growled in reply.

She ignored him and scooted away from the potted trees to flatten herself against the house.

Rather than follow and be hugely conspicuous, he guarded, sniffing the air for approaching guards or inhabitants. He got the occasional tickle of something that teased his olfactory sense, but nothing concrete.

Whoosh.

He whipped his head around to see only the flash of Penny as she went inside the house and slid the door shut. What the fuck?

Screw hiding, he went right to the glass and nosed it. He couldn't open it in this shape, but a naked ginger would be even more noticeable than an oversized fox.

Goddammit!

He was just about to say fuck it and charge in after her when the door slipped open and Penny emerged. She mouthed, "Let's go."

She moved back to the fence, which was where they ran into the dilemma of how to get back over.

Easy enough for her. He shifted and almost chuckled as she immediately averted her gaze. He cupped his hands. She stepped into them, and he hoisted her enough so she could flip to the other side.

Now for him. He eyed the stone wall and its electrified spikes. He gripped the edge of the fence and pulled himself up, doing his best to keep to his tiny sliver of free space. But there just wasn't enough room to give him—

ZZZZT.

He blinked as a wet shirt hit the barbs and shorted the line. Lights came on. Shouts sounded in the distance, and she whispered, "Quick. Get over here."

He scrambled over the fence even as he feared they couldn't truly escape, but it appeared she'd thought of a plan for that as well.

Naked in the pool, she was the one to break off the kiss as the homeowners gaped at them.

The security guard from next door barked into his walkie, "False alarm. Just skinny-dippers."

SIXTEEN

KIT DIDN'T SAY MUCH AS THEY WALKED BACK TO their rental, him shirtless because she'd ruined hers shorting out the fence.

Worth it. Especially the part where she'd dragged him into the water with her, wearing only her panties and bra after quickly removing her shoes and pants.

It had proved to be the perfect cover, with the elderly homeowners screeching about the perverts in their pool then yelling at the guard for trespassing into their yard. There was talk of calling the police, but oddly enough, the security guy was the one to persuade the older folks to let them off with a warning.

Wouldn't want to draw attention.

Kit held her hand, despite his ire. When they

were a block away, she finally said, "Unless Gerard has completely changed his scent, he's not the one living there."

He tensed then relaxed. "Good. I'll arrange for you to return home in the morning."

She stopped walking and dragged him to a stop too. "I'm not leaving."

"I only brought you here to see if it was the same guy. It's not. You're not needed."

He meant for the mission, but her heart didn't like it one bit. "I want to help."

"I don't need it."

"Never asked if you did. I am offering."

"No."

"Why?"

"Because whoever owns that house is obviously into something illegal that you shouldn't be involved with."

"But you should?" she queried.

"I'm trained for this."

"Now. You weren't always."

He glared at her. "This isn't a game, Penny."

She rather liked the nickname he'd given her, although she had to wonder if he thought of her as the good-luck or bad version. "You're right, it's not. This is serious stuff, and you want to know what? It feels good doing something about it, to act rather than wallow in fear."

"Act? Is that what we're calling your foolishness?"

She snorted. "You're just mad because my plan worked."

"Barely."

"But it did. We got inside, and I got a good enough sniff to tell you that, while Gerard doesn't live in that house, a Were did pass through."

"Are you sure?"

She nodded. "Wolf. Not one I recognized. Recent too."

"Only one scent?"

"Two, but I didn't get a good feel for the second one. I didn't go too far because I could hear people inside. But I did get a whiff of the kitchen and dining area, which I figured would be the most likely places people would congregate."

"Smart thinking." Grudging praise.

"The Were I got a good whiff of is female and sat at the dining table, indicating she isn't a prisoner."

"Maybe. Could be she was tied to the chair." His fingers linked with hers as they resumed walking.

"I didn't smell any blood or medical supplies." Both scents had been common where Gerard had held her prisoner.

"Doesn't mean shit, though. Could be the Were are kept locked in a sealed space, basement being the most likely. Or they're imprisoned off-site."

"How many addresses does this guy have?"

"He's renting just this one, but the company he's leasing from has a few. An office building, a golf club, and two warehouses, both on the up-and-up, according to quick online checks. But something like a medical lab for Were wouldn't be something they'd keep on the books."

"So what's our next move?"

"There is no 'our.' You're going home, remember?"

The impish smile she turned on him was one her older brother probably recalled from their youth. "No, I'm not, and you can't make me."

"Penny..." He groaned her name as they reached the front door of their rental.

"Yes, my sexy fox?"

"Why are you making this hard?"

Still feeling mischievous, she cupped him. "Want me to fix it?"

"I—"

Rather than hear another excuse, she kissed him and might have done more if the door hadn't opened and her brother hadn't glared. "About time you both got back. We have trouble."

Poppy wanted to throttle him, but the frazzled expression in his eyes stopped her. "What's wrong?"

"Get inside." Darian stepped onto the porch and glanced around suspiciously before entering after them and bolting the door.

"Spill it. What did you do?" Kit drawled.

"I didn't do shit. We have a visitor."

"Who?" Poppy asked, following him to the living room, where the woman who looked from afar an awful lot like her dead mother sat. In person, many other differences glared, but the most striking was her scent.

"Who are you? What are you doing here?" Kit growled, eyeing the woman, who rose from the chair to press against the wall in fear.

"Don't hurt me. I swear I don't mean any harm," the stranger exclaimed.

"Leash it, Kit," Poppy commanded as she went toward the woman, hands outstretched. "Don't be afraid. We won't hurt you."

"Speak for yourself," Kit muttered.

"Ignore him. I'm Poppy." She inclined her head. "And you are?"

"Rosemary." A low mumble.

"Hi, Rosemary. You look a little frightened. Why don't I make us a cup of tea and you can tell us why you've come to visit?"

She bit her lip. "I shouldn't be here. But I had to warn you."

"Warn us about what?" Kit snapped.

Rosemary recoiled.

Poppy soothed her. "Don't pay Kit any mind. The red hair makes him ornery. Come with me." She shot a glare at the men. "The boys can stay here while you and I chat."

They entered the kitchen, and once the door swung shut, she could no longer hear the agitated murmurs of the two guys.

She concentrated on their guest as she prepped the kettle and pulled out a plate for cookies.

"So tell me, Rosemary, are you part of the local Pack?" There was no denying her Were scent, the same one from the house she'd just infiltrated.

"I am. Was." She fidgeted, hands in her lap, head down. "My Pack's pretty much gone now."

"What happened?" Poppy stayed by the stove, knowing it wouldn't take long for the water to boil.

"I don't know what happened to them other than they started disappearing."

"Oh?" Poppy pretended ignorance. "Did they move away?"

"No. Someone took them." A darkly spoken claim.

"Who?" Poppy waited for Rosemary to admit it was the man she lived with.

The woman shrugged. "I don't know. But I got scared. Lucky for me, my boyfriend had room at his place for me to move in."

The story mimicked her mother's, which was why Poppy blurted out, "Is he the one behind their disappearance?"

Rosemary's shock was palpable. "Teddy? He'd never hurt a fly."

"Then why the guards and electrified spikes?" She realized too late that she'd revealed knowing where he lived and his security.

Rosemary didn't call her on it. "I guess your brother told you Teddy's got me living in his version of Fort Knox." Her smile held fondness as she added, "He takes such good care of me."

"Does Teddy know what you are?" Poppy approached the table with the tea.

Her eyes widened. "Gracious, no. He's human and not oath-bound, although I'm thinking I might get him to make the pledge. We're so perfect togeth-er." She sighed.

"If he doesn't know, then why all the security?" Poppy nudged.

"He thinks I used to belong to a gang." She giggled.

"Guess I kind of do. Or used to." Her lips turned down. "Ain't many of us left now. You're the first I've come across in weeks. Which is why I had to warn you. You should leave before someone makes you disappear too."

If Kit had been the one questioning this woman, Poppy knew he'd be suspicious about why she would care about strangers. But that would be because he considered himself coldhearted. Poppy found it more suspicious that this woman, whom they'd never met, had pegged them for Were.

"I'm glad for the warning, but don't worry. We can take care of ourselves."

"Who are those guys?" Rosemary's gaze slewed to the closed door.

"Brother and boyfriend." The best explanation. "We're here on vacation." Never mind this wasn't a tourist destination.

"You might want to think about finishing your trip somewhere else." Rosemary stood. "I should get going before Teddy gets worried. He thinks I ran out to get some ice cream."

Poppy bit her inner cheek before stating the obvious. If he was worried about her safety, would he really be letting her wander the neighborhood alone?

Apparently, Darian thought the same thing, so when they emerged from the kitchen, he had his shoes on and said, "Let me walk you home."

"Aren't you just a gentleman?" Rosemary offered a girlish giggle.

They left, and Poppy waited for Kit to say something. When he didn't, she sighed. "Before you say anything, I know she's lying."

"Oh?" Only a single syllable.

"She does live with Kline. Her scent was the one in that kitchen. But she lied when she claimed she doesn't know what's happened to her Pack."

Kit held up his phone. "While you were chatting, I ran her name against the last list we had for the local Pack. Guess who's not on it? As a matter of fact, no one named Rosemary is in any of our databases."

"Meaning what?"

"I don't know, only that it's odd that an unregistered Were has ended up in a place where others have gone missing."

"How do we find out who she is?"

"I'd say that's less important than why she suddenly showed up on our doorstep, because I don't believe for a second she came here to warn us."

"Then what?"

"Scouting. Finding out why we're here, how many. Probably trying to determine how hard we'd be to take down."

The declaration had her yelling, "And you let

Darian leave with her!" She bolted for the front door, but Kit grabbed her.

"Slow down."

"He's in danger."

"No more than you were when you chose to jump that fence."

She scowled at him. "My brother better not get hurt."

He smirked. "He said the same thing when you and I went for our walk."

For some reason, his smugness annoyed her, and she shoved him. He didn't move, but he did arch a brow.

"Feel better?"

"No," she grumbled.

"Would it help if I said I won't allow your brother to be harmed? Or you?"

"You can't promise that. For all you know, that woman killed Darian or drugged him or—"

"He's back."

Her brother entered, exclaiming, "That woman hit on me!"

And Poppy burst into tears.

SEVENTEEN

PENNY GOT OVER HER EMOTIONAL OUTBURST quickly as her brother mocked her.

"I knew you loved me. And to reinforce that, you should bake me some cookies!" Darian declared.

"I was worried!" Penny yelled and smacked her brother, which caused some surprise. Kit knew she wasn't usually violent, but since coming on this trip, he'd noticed she was flinching less and being more outspoken.

"He's fine. I want to know what he learned from the woman."

"Other than she's a con artist?" Darian stated with an arch of his brow.

"What makes you say that?" Penny asked.

Kit had known from the start that there was something off about Rosemary.

"She came on to me right away, despite telling me about her wonderful boyfriend." Darian rolled his eyes.

"Maybe she's into younger guys?" Kit played devil's advocate.

"Seems unlikely." Penny shook her head. "She told me in the kitchen she thought Kline was her soul mate and that he saved her. She also claimed he's not behind the disappearances."

Darian snorted. "She lied."

"She sounded sincere." Penny, though, seemed uncertain about her impression.

"That woman was playing us." Kit agreed with Darian's conclusion. "Obviously, our target is aware of our presence and sent her to gather intel.

"You think he already connected us to the skinny-dipping incident?" she asked.

"Wait, what?"" Darian exclaimed. "Is that why my sister showed up soaking wet and wearing your clothes?" Something that had been ignored in the confusion of having a visitor.

"Don't be a prude. At least I found a way to get a sniff inside the house," Penny casually dropped.

"You did what?" Darian bellowed.

"Calm down. What I did wasn't any worse than you being nice to that woman and then walking her home."

"You allowed this?" Darian growled at Kit, who lifted his hands.

"Don't blame me for the fact your sister is headstrong."

"I'm not as fragile as you both think," she retorted.

Perhaps not, but Kit wanted to treat her as if she were.

"With our cover blown, should we move?" Darian asked.

"You and Penelope should go home."

Darian and his sister replied in tandem, "Like fuck."

A sigh escaped Kit as he raked his fingers through his hair. "This might get dangerous for you both."

"We're not leaving you alone!" Penny hotly declared.

"Gonna have to share the glory, foxy." Darian winked.

Kit might finally snap, but it appeared he was stuck with the pair of them.

When they went to bed—her to the master bedroom, alone, and Darian taking the other room—Kit propped himself on the couch and called Luna.

"Shouldn't you be in bed?" she said without a hello.

"Don't you want an update?" was his riposte.

"Is it him?"

"No."

"I hear a but."

He glanced at the covered window. "There's something not quite right. We met the suspect's girl-friend. A Were, not from the local Pack, and yet, she lied about it and said she belonged. She did admit to knowing about the disappearances, but she's claiming she doesn't know what's happening. Gave us a warning to leave."

"You think she's being coerced into giving up our kind?"

"I don't know what her angle is, but I am thinking a meeting with her boyfriend is in order."

"Are you still thinking of sending Poppy in as bait?"

"No." He should have never even suggested that. "Given this Kline isn't Gerard, I'm going to talk to the man myself."

"I thought he was heavily guarded."

"At home. I was planning something a little more public."

"Be careful, Kit. That bad feeling is getting worse."

"Maybe you should see a doctor. You're not getting any younger."

She snorted. "I can still whup your ass. So don't test me."

As if she'd ever hurt him. She'd taught him to fight, but she'd never used her strength or ability to hurt him. Punishment came via her disappointment, never her fists.

In her words, *You should only ever do violence to protect yourself or others, never as correction.* Which actually flew in the face of most Pack tendencies, where might trumped wits.

But then again, Luna always was different from everyone else, and not just because of her eyes.

He ended the call with her and tried to get comfortable on the couch. It didn't have room to stretch, so he flopped to the floor and sighed.

"Can't sleep either?" Penny's soft query startled him.

How had he not heard her coming? Blame the fact he'd not been himself since meeting her.

He sat up. "What's wrong?"

"Would you believe I feel guilty about having that big bed to myself while you get a shitty couch?"

His lips twitched. "I've slept on worse."

She sat down beside him. "The bed is big enough for two."

The offer tempted. Sanity prevailed. "I can't."

"Why?"

He blurted out the truth. "I don't know if I could keep myself from touching you."

"Good, because I want you to touch me."

The admission almost blew his resolve away. His dick was ready to go, but he tried to find an excuse. "Your brother would be pissed."

"It's none of his business who I invite into my bed." She leaned closer. "And make no mistake, I am inviting you. I want you, Kit. Touching me. Kissing me. Inside me."

He closed his eyes. "Stop."

"Why should I? I know you want me too."

"I do." He admitted his weakness.

She took his hand. "You protest way too much."

"I'm—"

"Less broken than me. So don't even think of using that as an excuse."

What he wanted to actually say was he was not worthy, but he had a feeling she'd ignore the protest. When she tugged him to his feet, he couldn't resist anymore. He didn't just stand, he swept her into his arms, knowing this moment would change everything.

And he didn't care.

He carried her to the master bedroom, closing the door and locking it, despite knowing that wouldn't stop a determined boot.

He laid her on the bed and was aware she watched as he peeled off his shirt. She wore a long shirt. His, as a matter of fact. Did she crave his scent as much as he craved hers?

It would make sense. She'd called him her mate.

And she was his.

Fuck me. After tonight, there'd be no denying it, no going back.

"Are you sure?"

She reached for him. "Shut up and kiss me."

He couldn't say no. Her eyes closed as he pressed his lips against hers. No denying something electric existed between them. He just had to see her, think of her, scent her, and he ignited with desire.

His kiss grew demanding, the slant of his mouth over hers coaxing, caressing, and her mouth parted for the sinuous slide of his tongue. He felt her shiver as his body settled against hers.

Peppering her with sensual kisses, he left her mouth to follow the line of her jaw. When he found the lobe of her ear and sucked it, she uttered a soft cry and arched.

He hushed her. "Shh. We don't need someone interrupting us."

She grabbed his hand and used his fingers as a chew toy, nibbling them and then biting down as his lips burned a trail down the column of her throat, nipping at her skin. Her pulse pounded as hard as his. Her flesh heated, but no more than his.

Her lower body pressed into him, seeking the pressure only he could give. He ground into her, rotating and thrusting despite their clothes. She undulated under him, moving in time with his motions, driving him wild.

He claimed another kiss, the taste of her intoxicating. By leaning to one side, braced on an elbow, he could skim her flesh, his fingers sliding under the fabric of the shirt and her bra, finding her bare breast, the peak of it already a hard point. His thumb brushed over it, and she caught a moan, strangling it.

She arched off the bed when he bent to capture the tip of her breast, still covered by fabric. He tugged at the nipple, sucked it through the bra, growling against her flesh as she shuddered and wiggled on the bed.

He wanted more. His shirt got removed and tossed. The bra too. He then attacked her breasts with his mouth and hands, teasing and sucking, pinching and fondling. Her fingers threaded through his hair and gripped as he enjoyed teasing her, delighting in every gasp and shiver.

It wasn't enough. He needed to taste her. Savor the honey he could smell. It tantalized. His lips blazed a path down her torso to the thin scrap of her panties. He hooked his fingers in them and yanked them off, freeing her to his touch and gaze.

With his face this close to her mound, he was immersed in her mouthwatering scent. He couldn't resist and buried his face between her legs.

"Oh." The exclamation was soft as he blew hotly against her. He positioned her so her legs draped over his shoulders, exposing her to him, allowing him to indulge in some sweet honey. He was in heaven with the first lick. He hummed as he kept licking and tasting, his contented growl a teasing vibration against her moist flesh.

He took his time lapping and teasing as he tugged her clit with his lips, played with it until she went tense, her climax on the brink.

He helped her along by thrusting two fingers inside her and then flicking her clit over and over with his tongue. Lick. Finger-fuck. Suck. Thrust. She tightened, and her panting emerged mixed with mewls of need.

He understood that need. He throbbed, wanted nothing more than to bury himself inside her. But this first time, he wanted her to come first. And she did.

Gloriously, muffling her cry with a fist to her mouth, her body arching and shuddering. Her channel clenched at his fingers as she rippled with pleasure.

Only when her pleasure had eased did she tug at him.

"Kiss me!" she demanded. She didn't seem to care if her honey was still on his lips.

She clung to him, her legs locked loosely around his waist as she reached between them to fiddle with his pants. "Your turn."

He just had to say, "Are you sure?" Even as he knew they'd already gone too far.

"Shut up and fuck me."

The vulgar words from her lips had him groaning and helping her to strip off his clothes. The tip of him found the entrance to her sex, and he thrust into her.

"Yes!" she hissed, digging her nails into his shoulders. "Yes." She kept saying it as he pumped into her, deep and hard. His hands on her ass tilted her so that he could keep fucking her at that sweet angle that made her tighten.

He'd found her G-spot and kept butting against it. She soon rocked in time with him, her body coiling as she rushed toward a second climax. A good thing she was close, because he was about to lose it. The suction of her sex on his cock had him ready to cream.

He buried his face into the soft curve of her neck and sucked the flesh as he pumped into her faster, slamming in and out of her, hearing her pant and cry out. Her nails dug into him as she arched.

He hoped she marked him. Wanted her to claim him.

When she came, he followed, his last thrust putting him deep as she shuddered all around him, satisfying him in a way he'd never imagined.

Joining them in a bond that would last for as long as they both lived.

They were mated. He didn't need the change in her scent to feel it.

Know it.

She's mine.

And he'd kill anyone who ever tried to take her away.

EIGHTEEN

HE'S MINE.

The thought reverberated through her head, and body, even Poppy's soul. The certainty had her smiling and smug as she left the bed where Kit slept, looking peaceful for once.

She practically skipped down the stairs, wearing a stupidly wide smile her brother noticed the moment he walked into the kitchen later.

"Ew. Gross. Ugh." He gagged.

"What's wrong?" she asked brightly as she turned from the stove, where she fried bacon.

"I can't believe you slept with that ginger. Have you forgotten he's an enforcer?"

She waved the spatula at him. "Don't you talk about my mate like that."

"Not your mate. Say it isn't so," Darian groaned.

"He is, and you will be nice about it or else."

"Depends. Or else what?" A sly query.

"No more cupcakes with butter cream frosting for you."

Aghast at the thought, he dropped his jaw. "Now that's just plain mean. See how being mated to him has already changed you? You used to be a nice sister," he grumbled.

"Still nice, but I won't tolerate anyone trash-talking my mate." She loved saying it aloud, and Kit heard her words as he entered the kitchen.

For a moment, he froze, his expression stiff.

Too soon? Too bad. Her smile held welcome as she said, "It's a beautiful day." In her mind. The overcast sky outside might indicate otherwise.

"Ha," Darian snorted.

Kit glanced at her brother, his expression flat, while the look on Darian's face dared him to do something about his disrespect.

The corner of her mate's mouth lifted. "It is a beautiful fucking day." He then deliberately walked over to Poppy and dropped a kiss on her lips, murmuring, "Morning, gorgeous."

The *gorgeous* was a nice touch, but that peck? Too little. She flung her arms around his neck and gave him a proper embrace, which had Darian gagging for real. By the time she ended the kiss, they both huffed a little, and his eyes held that shine that happened only around her.

"Your morning is about to get even better. Sit, so I can fill your belly," she ordered and pointed. Once Kit leaned back in his chair, she proceeded to feed the two most important men in her life, which some feminists might decry. Let them. Poppy derived true pleasure out of cooking for others, of hearing their happy eating noises and seeing them clear their plates.

She cooked, but she rarely had to clean up afterward. Darian and Kit insisted she go for her shower while they handled it. Luckily, it didn't take them long, and she soon had company.

Kit entered the steamy bathroom and almost shyly said, "Need someone to wash your back?"

"I'd rather you made me dirty," was her reply. Apparently, he'd rather as well. They used up the whole tank of hot water, and she didn't regret it one bit.

As they dressed, she asked, "So what's the plan for today?" With all that had happened the previous day, she expected things would keep moving rapidly.

"I'm going to force a face-to-face meeting with Kline." He put on a tie.

"How are you going to manage that? His place is guarded. He likely won't just let you in."

"I'm not going to his house. I'm going to watch and wait to see where he goes today. If I'm lucky, he'll go somewhere public, like a restaurant."

"Your plan is to follow him around, hoping he'll go somewhere where you can confront him?" Her incredulity shone. He might be her mate, but she saw flaws in his plan.

"You don't think that will work?"

"Even if you do manage to ask him some questions, he's not likely to admit he's involved in a nefarious plot to capture Were."

"I can be persuasive," Kit declared.

"Please, we both know you're not the cajoling, sweet-talking type."

He arched a brow. "You might have a point. Skip the nice talk, go right to the threats."

"If you're going to hit him, be sure to do it out of the public eye," she admonished, even as she didn't discourage him from whatever methods he'd have to use. Another person might have been squeamish about the violence, but she knew Kline posed a grave danger to their kind. There could be no leniency.

The Were secret was more important than a few bruises, broken bones, or loose teeth. Even the death of one human paled in comparison with the likely genocide if humanity discovered their existence. When they'd been discovered in the past, it had always resulted in humanity trying to eliminate all Were. They'd worked hard to play down the werewolves in history texts in favor of highlighting the persecution of witches. Ask someone today which more likely existed, witch or werewolf, chances were they'd claim the first.

They'd be wrong. Or so she'd been led to believe. At times, Poppy wondered if witches, like Were, simply chose to not exist outside their own kind. Did they have their own kind of oath to protect them from outsiders?

"Hitting is for amateurs," Kit said. "Applying pressure in the proper place is much more effective."

She shivered, though she wasn't frightened by his words. She should have been somewhat repelled, but the strength in him, the way he took charge, thrilled her.

"What if he's a dupe?"

"Even if he's the smallest cog in the disappearances, he knows too much. But I won't eliminate him until he's given us everything he can."

"Be careful." She moved into his arms and put her head on his chest.

He wrapped his arms around her. "Don't worry, Penny. I've been doing this for a while. I know how to stay safe. I'm more worried about you. Promise me you'll stay in the house while I'm gone."

She leaned back enough to see his eyes. Full of worry. She wanted to ease the tension between his brows. Only... She couldn't fall into the trap she had with her brother and Pack. Time to be strong. "Sorry, I can't promise that."

His eyes widened. "What's that supposed to mean?"

"I'm not a child who needs coddling. Nor will I be a prisoner of my own fear, or yours."

"I'm not locking you up. Just asking you to stay inside while I'm gone."

She cupped his cheeks. "I'll be okay."

"The danger—"

"Is just as great for you as it is for me. Should I tell you to stay here and cower?"

His lips pressed tight.

She kept going. "And who says I'm safe inside this house? Kline knows we're here. If he's not the type to do the dirty work himself, we can't predict who will show up or when."

"I should stay with you."

"You are not neglecting your job because we just mated, and you're feeling überprotective."

"I can't help myself." He moved from her, fists clenched at his sides. "It's entirely unreasonable. After all the criticism I've heaped on you, saying that you've been hiding behind others, here I am trying to do the same."

"Because you care. That's not a bad thing."

He stood facing the wall. Rigid. "For the first time, I'm not sure what to do."

Two steps and Poppy could place a hand on his broad back. "You will do your job. You're going to follow Kline and have a chat with him. But to ease your mind, I will promise to not leave this house without Darian." Too much pride and stubbornness encouraged stupidity. She shouldn't dismiss Kit's valid fears. Were disappeared in this place.

"I guess that's okay," was his reluctant reply. "But only because I know your brother would die before letting anyone harm a hair on your head."

"Everything will be fine." She'd spoken softly as she kissed him. Now if only she believed her own lie.

A knot of unease plagued her stomach as Kit left, determined to confront Kline.

Darian stood by her side as they watched him driving off in the clunky truck. Not exactly inconspicuous.

A chill had her shivering, and she hugged herself. "I've got a bad feeling." Maybe she should have insisted on joining him.

"The fucker is sly. He'll be fine," her brother replied as he put an arm around her.

She busied herself baking as she waited for Kit's texts. He kept her apprised.

Down the street. No movement.

The batter she whipped up had a few substitutions, given the less-than-ideal range of ingredients in the house.

As she put the muffins in the oven, the next ding had her tripping to get to her phone.

Sedan just left. Following.

She wandered from the kitchen, timer set on her phone, and found her brother, who pored over Kit's laptop.

"What are you looking for?"

"Information. Your mate has some files on the situation that make for interesting reading."

"What did you find?" she asked, faking interest as she peered out the window as if she'd see Kit driving down the street.

"This isn't the first Pack to disappear. He's got folders, some dating back decades."

"Decades?" She blinked. "And the Lykosium are just noticing now?"

"Can't blame them. Not one of those Packs ever reported anything amiss. They just fizzled away."

"Like ours did," she muttered. "Are the same people behind it?"

"Doesn't say. But I do know Kline isn't really old

enough to be responsible for ours getting wiped out. He'd have been, like, ten at the time."

"Gerard would have been old enough," she said through stiff lips.

Darian grabbed her cold hands and squeezed. "If he's alive, we'll find him. We won't let him get away with this."

She indulged in his comfort and promise for a moment before exclaiming, "We should be doing something."

"We are. We're studying the case." He waved to the laptop.

"We've already been over it. We need new information. New clues." As she paced in tight back-and-forth lengths, it hit her. "Kline's left the house, but Rosemary might still be there."

"And?"

"If pressed properly, she might have more to say about her boyfriend's activities."

"I thought we decided she was lying."

"We did. Why is she lying, though? We have to find out." Once the idea took hold, it strengthened.

"Find out how? She didn't leave a phone number."

"We're going to pay her a visit. I wonder if she likes muffins."

"I don't think so. That's way too dangerous.

Besides, I told your ginger I'd keep you inside where it's safe."

She glared at Darian. "I'd like to see you try."

"Now, Poppy Seed, don't be difficult."

She might have gone off on him if her phone hadn't buzzed with a text.

At a golf club. Kline appears to be stopping for lunch.

He also dropped a pin to give her a location. She sent back a heart emoji.

Then a peach. Then an eggplant.

"I take it the ginger is okay?"

"He's perfect. Now, are you coming with me or not?" She turned off her timer as she asked. As the muffins cooled on a rack, she changed clothes and brushed her hair. Darian sighed quite a bit, taking lessons from Kit, as she packed the warm muffins in a tin.

Together, they headed down the sidewalk toward Kline's property. In minutes, they stood outside the gate. She pressed a red button.

The video monitor remained dark, but a voice barked, "What do you want?"

Poppy held up the treats. "Just popping by to say hi to Rosemary with some freshly made muffins."

"Who are you?"

"I'm Poppy Smith, and this is my brother,

Darian. We're friends of hers. Could you tell her we're here? I'm sure she'll want to say hello." Poppy offered the camera her most innocuous smile, not the least bit scared, oddly enough. How could she be in broad daylight, her brother by her side, while Kit was off confronting the probable villain?

The monitor didn't speak again, but the gate did buzz and click as the latch released. The gate rolled to the side, admitting them to the property.

A step inside, she saw no sign of the guard with the gun, but Poppy's nape prickled. She sensed they were being watched. She could also smell several different distinct people. More than she liked. She should have asked Kit how many people had left with Kline.

Or had the man driven himself?

Darian mumbled, "This might have been a bad idea."

While Poppy agreed, she didn't say so aloud. "It will be fine."

"It better be, or your boyfriend will rearrange my face."

"Be ready to turn on the charm," she muttered as the door to the house swung open, framing Rosemary.

She wore yoga capris and a tank top that showed off her braless state, her nipples unabashedly poking the fabric. Her golden hair, rather than in loose waves, was pulled back today in a high ponytail. Her makeup appeared immaculate. She was also barefoot, smelled of cigarettes, and...

Darian was the one to hiss, "She doesn't smell like a wolf."

Indeed, today her scent was comprised of a lilac fragrance and human. How was that even possible?

As they neared the door, Poppy faked a bright smile and held up the muffins. "I brought a freshly baked treat."

"How sweet. Won't you come in?" Rosemary's polite reply didn't raise any hairs on her body, and yet, the tension in her gut tightened.

Entering the house proved confusing, because, this time, there were no Were scents at all. Only human. Even the kitchen that Rosemary led them to, with its massive gleaming island and stools, held no Were scents. How was that possible? She'd scented two Were the night before.

"What the fuck is going on?" Darian didn't bother hiding his curiosity beneath a polite veneer.

"What do you mean?" Rosemary asked, the innocence ruined by a smirk.

Poppy's lips pursed as she placed the muffins on the counter. "Drop the act. We know you're a liar, not to mention human. You faked your Were scent."

"That's impossible—" Darian started, only to be interrupted by Rosemary's laughter.

"You animals and your sniffing thing. I didn't believe Teddy when he said it was that simple, but lo and behold, a little wolf perfume, and poof, you idiots just welcome me into your canine club."

The implication stunned Poppy. "You infiltrated the local Pack."

"It was so easy. Give them a sob story about being a loner preyed upon by other loners and they bend over backward to bring you in."

Poppy's eyes widened. "You lured those missing people by making them think you were one of them."

It was Darian who spotted the hole. "How do you know who's Were and who isn't?"

"Because you have a mole who was more than happy to give us a starting point in exchange for bitcoin. Turns out your kind is just as greedy as humans."

"Who?" Who would do that? Poppy couldn't wrap her mind around it.

"As if I'd tell."

"More like you don't know," Darian declared. "You're just the hired help."

The statement surprised Poppy, until Rosemary snapped, "I'm his partner. We pulled off the extractions together."

With that confirmation, Poppy's rage exploded. "What have you done to them?"

"Me? Nothing. My job is to get them to lower their guard for capture. What happens after is none of my business."

Darian bristled, fists clenched at his sides. "Don't lie. You know why your boyfriend wants them."

"You're the one who is wrong. Teddy has no interest in your furry friends. It's all about the money. He's what you might call a procurement specialist for those seeking a unique experience."

Poppy didn't even want to know what that meant. Her stomach turned.

"You won't get away with this. The Lykosium are on to you," Darian warned.

That brought laughter to Rosemary's lips. "More like we're on to your precious council. Where do you think the leak came from? It's how we knew you were in town. I'll admit I thought you'd be harder to capture, but here you are, just putting yourself in my hands."

"Tell me who!" Darian lunged, but not quickly enough for the athletic Rosemary, who leaped out of the way with a laugh.

"Don't even bother, wolfman. I've got four armed guards waiting to take you into custody."

"You won't get away with this," Poppy declared. "Kit knows we're here."

"The redhead? The big boss was most excited when he saw a picture of him. Teddy promised to bring him in and was delighted when he saw him skulking around earlier. As we speak, Teddy has probably already captured your friend."

Ice flowed into her veins as Poppy whispered, "No."

"Any second now, I imagine Teddy will text me to let me know he's been tagged and relocated."

"Relocated where? Where is he taking Kit?" Poppy went to dive on the woman, ready to throttle for answers, only to freeze when Rosemary pulled a gun from behind the counter.

"Don't move. Or move and die. Your choice."

"You're going to shoot us both?"

"One for sure, which will bring the guards. The question is, who should I shoot? And just so you're aware, I already know from experience that blood mops up nicely on this floor."

"Better have good aim, because if you don't kill me, you'll die two seconds after," Poppy threatened.

"She doesn't mean that." Darian raised his hands. "Don't shoot."

His acquiescence had Poppy glaring at him. "What are you doing?"

"Protecting you from getting shot."

"She's going to do worse if she captures us!" Her veins ran hot and cold at the thought.

"Trust me."

Poppy might have argued, but she trusted her brother implicitly. He must have a plan.

Rosemary appeared triumphant as she said aloud to her home-monitoring system, "Alfred, send security to the kitchen."

An AI replied, "At once, ma'am."

As the seconds ticked by, Poppy's anxiety grew. Kit needed her while they wasted time with this psycho. But how to get out of this without getting shot?

The thump of feet preceded the appearance of two men, neither in uniform.

"Who are you? Where's Derrick and Gavin?" Rosemary demanded.

Hammer arched a brow as he sauntered into the room. "You mean those meatheads having a nap in the garden? I'd fire them for sleeping on the job."

The gun swiveled toward Hammer. "Get out of my house!"

"Not without my friends." Hammer crossed his arms.

"Another dog. My lucky day," Rosemary

sneered, obviously dumber than she looked, because one gun wouldn't stop three Were.

But three Were could distract her as Lochlan snuck up behind Rosemary and wrapped an arm around her, drawing her aiming arm down and rendering the gun harmless.

"Did no one ever tell you it's not nice to shoot people bearing muffins?" Lochlan grumbled.

"I thought I smelled Poppy's cooking." Hammer ignored Rosemary and turned his attention to the fresh-baked goods.

"We don't have time for this!" Poppy exclaimed. "Kit's in danger." She sent him a text. *Get out. It's a trap.* But he didn't reply.

Darian took charge. "Lochlan, secure this woman and the house while we go after the enforcer."

"You won't get away with this!" Rosemary's cry was shrill.

"Ha, we've been getting away with all kinds of shit for longer than the history books can remember," Hammer declared.

Rosemary screeched, "I'll fucking—" Lochlan cut her off by placing his hand over her mouth.

"You sure we need to keep her alive?" he complained.

"Yes. She knows about the missing Were." Even admitting it soured Poppy's mouth.

While Lochlan secured Rosemary, Hammer, a muffin in each hand, followed them out of the house.

He had the keys to the car and insisted on hearing their story as he drove.

At the end of the recap, Hammer whistled. "The humans have found a way to mimic Were scent. That's not good."

"Not really surprising, given we already knew the Lykosium enforcers can camouflage theirs," Darian added. That was how they made such good spies.

"What the fuck is this Kline fellow capturing Were for, though?" Hammer asked the most pertinent question.

"More important, how could anyone actually be selling us out? The Lykosium are supposed to protect. If we can't trust them..." Darian's words trailed off, because they all knew. If the Lykosium couldn't be trusted, they were well and truly screwed. Poppy wondered whether those other Packs had been decimated because of treachery.

"How did you find us?" Darian finally asked as Hammer blew through a yellow light that was red before they finished crossing the intersection.

"Followed my nose." Hammer tapped the side of it. "Car got fixed quicker than expected. We were coming up the street as you guys were leaving, so we thought we'd follow. Keep an eye on you. Good thing we did."

A good thing indeed.

Their timing couldn't have been better.

Unfortunately, they'd wasted too much time with Rosemary, because they arrived at the golf club too late.

Teddy and Kit were already gone.

NINETEEN

Kᴉᴛ ᴛᴀᴘᴘᴇᴅ ᴛʜᴇ sᴛᴇᴇʀɪɴɢ ᴡʜᴇᴇʟ ᴏf ᴛʜᴇ ᴛʀᴜᴄᴋ as he watched Teddy, a thickset man, though in a way that indicated muscle, not fat, enter the golf club restaurant.

Something nagged at him. And it wasn't just the fact he'd left his new mate alone, close to enemy territory.

The whole situation stank, which was when it hit him. Rosemary's scent. Wolf. Of that, he had no doubt, but it occurred to him that he'd not once scented her in the garden. Not by the pool or the patio. Surely the woman spent some time outdoors. He'd caught several human aromas, but no wolves.

Did that mean something? His hand went to the ignition, and he was about to start the truck and return to Poppy when a slick town car with tinted windows pulled into the parking lot. Rather than stop under the portico, it drove around to the side.

The car might not be related to Teddy's appearance. Still... He'd come to do a job. He'd feel stupid later if he squandered this opportunity over irrational panic.

Especially since she'd texted him back right away. With emojis.

He tucked the phone away and got out of the truck. Glad he'd worn his tie today, Kit swaggered into the club and stopped by the maître d' at the door, who eyed him up and down. "The dining room is for members only."

Kit slid him a hundred-dollar bill. "I'll just be a minute. I need to speak to Mr. Kline."

To his surprise, the man wouldn't take the bribe. "My job is worth more than petty cash."

"Tell you what, why don't you ask Mr. Kline if he'd like to speak with me? Tell him the council sent me."

Anyone who dealt with Were, even a human stealing them, would have heard that term. And if they were smart, they feared it.

The maître d' pursed his lips but took the bill and wandered into the dining room. He returned shortly and inclined his head.

"Mr. Kline has invited you to join him and his guests."

Guests? That wasn't ideal. The man would be cagier in front of his cronies.

As Kit began to follow the snotty waiter, a scent, familiar and yet not, hit him. It tickled his memories, and for a second, he flashed to his past.

The hand reached into the cage and dragged him out by the scruff of the neck. He dangled in front of a smirking male, the scent of him bringing terror to his little body. This was the hunter who'd killed his mother and captured him.

Kit cleared his throat. "Where's your washroom?" Before waiting for a reply, he veered away and headed for the corridor discreetly labeled Ladies and Gents. This club for the rich had individual washrooms, which meant he could lock himself inside one and take a moment to breathe.

Still, he reeled. How could this be? The man responsible for the murder of his family had died decades ago. Yet he recognized the smell. He'd never forget it.

If the hunter lived, then someone had lied.

He splashed water on his face before he called Luna and barked, "What the fuck? He's not dead."

"Who's not dead?" was her reply.

"The hunter. The one who kept me in a cage."

There was dead silence on the other end before she whispered, "Are you sure it's him?"

"Pretty fucking sure. Care to explain how that's possible?"

"It shouldn't be. Everyone present that day on the hunt was exterminated."

"I hear a but."

"My after-action report indicated a car left the premises as the hunt began."

He racked his memories, trying to remember if those who'd chased him had included the one who'd caged him. He'd been so young. So frightened. "You mean to say, after all this time, that the bastard who killed my mother, my siblings, might still be alive?"

"We assumed whoever escaped got the message, given what happened to the other hunters."

"You thought wrong," he growled. "He's here. Now. And he's probably the one in cahoots with fucking Kline."

"Get out of there," Luna exclaimed. "Grab the Feral Pack wolves you brought and leave. Now. That's an order."

"You know I can't do that."

"This situation is more complex than we imagined."

"This situation needs to be resolved."

"Then wait for reinforcements."

"Doing that means those already taken captive might die."

"They're probably already dead," she snarled. "And you will be, too, if you don't listen to me."

"We're in a public place. I'll be fine." Physically, maybe, but mentally, he reeled.

"Kit—"

He cut her off. "This is my job. Remember? Protect the Were secret at all costs."

"Your life isn't worth it."

He uttered a short, derisive laugh. "Of all the Were, my life is the most dispensable. I'll call you later." He hung up and ignored the call when she called back. He put the phone on silent and slid it into his pocket. He grimaced at his reflection in the mirror over the sink.

Should he walk away? Yesterday, it would have been easy to forge ahead. After all, who cared about the life of an abomination? But today, he'd woken mated to a woman who needed him. Losing Kit would break her.

But more than that, he couldn't just let these assholes get away with their actions.

What to do?

When he exited, he had his phone in camera mode. Luna was right. He couldn't fuck this up, not with Penny so close by. He'd grab a few pictures and then meet up with his mate and her brother to form a better plan of attack.

He opened the bathroom door to see a man, older but wearing the same smarmy smile.

"We meet again, fox."

Before Kit could react, someone to his left jabbed him. A glance to his side showed Teddy pushing the plunger. Kit reacted by punching him, but not before most of the drug squirted into his system.

A poke from the other side came from another henchman armed with a needle. All the while, the hunter stood watching, smug, as he said, "What do you say we finish the hunt you ruined all those years ago?"

TWENTY

THE OLD TRUCK WAS IN THE PARKING LOT OF THE golf club. However, Kit couldn't be found, despite a thorough search of the premises. Not an easy thing to do, given that the pompous ass manning the reservation desk had threatened to call the police.

Hammer leaned on the podium and drawled, "You go right ahead, pinhead. You call the cops, and then you can explain to them why you're serving shark fin soup. Which is a major crime, by the way. As is any kind of bushmeat. And is it just me, or do I smell sea turtle too?"

The man, name-tagged Corey, blanched. "I don't know what you're talking about. We only have beef and chicken on the menu."

"I know my red meat and poultry, and that ain't what you're serving." Hammer spoke nicely, his tone at odds with his steely gaze. "I wonder how many years you'll get as an accessory for illegal trafficking and consumption of protected wildlife."

Corey's lips turned down, and he stopped trying to dial the phone. "The guy you're looking for is gone."

"Gone where?" Poppy asked a little too desperately.

The guy shrugged. "Don't know. Just that he came here looking to talk to Mr. Kline. He went to the bathroom and never came back."

Meaning he'd been jumped.

Darian had the foresight to ask, "Who was Kline meeting?"

When Corey hesitated, Hammer offered him an awful smile.

Corey gave up the goods. "I don't know his name, only that he's important. He comes in through the VIP entrance and meets with Mr. Kline every other month. Today, they didn't stay to eat. Left around the time your friend went missing."

"Describe Kline's lunch companion."

Corey launched into a vague description. The fellow appeared to be in his fifties or early sixties with short, salt-and-pepper hair. He was well-spoken, if a salty dick to staff.

As the group emerged from the golf club,

Poppy's shoulders slumped. Darian put his arm around her.

"We'll find him."

She wished she had his optimism. "How?" she murmured. And then it hit her. "His tracking chips! Luna will know how to find him."

"She probably could," Darian said. "The problem is getting a hold of her. The Lykosium isn't exactly big on being directly contacted. My understanding is there's some archaic system to leave them a message, and then you're supposed to wait to hear back."

That quickly, her hope sank. They couldn't afford to wait. They needed to contact Luna right now, and the only person who might know how? Rok. After all, Luna had been the one to elevate him to Alpha and give them declared-Pack status.

She put in a call to her Alpha as Darian drove them back to Kline's house. She quickly explained the situation to Rok, cut him off when he ranted, and then thanked him as he said, "I'll try and get a hold of Luna."

"You have her number?"

"No, but the Lykosium did give me a way to contact them in case of emergency."

As she hung up, it occurred to her how useless it was to have a group tasked with protecting them that couldn't be contacted in a timely fashion to do so.

The gates to Kline's property were open, and they drove right in. Lochlan sat on the front steps and looked annoyed. As usual.

As they piled out of the cars, sans Kit, Lochlan growled, "She's in the study."

Darian nodded. "Thanks. Watch Poppy, would you, while I have a talk with Rosemary."

"I'm coming with you," she insisted, which led to all the men saying, "No."

She crossed her arms. "Why not?"

"Because." Darian's dumb reply.

"I'm not stupid. I know you'll probably have to hurt her to get her to divulge her secrets."

"Then you understand why we don't want you watching."

She did understand. They thought her incapable of handling it.

Too fragile.

Too broken.

Too weak.

And she had been for a while, but now...

"I am not hiding anymore," she yelled. She shot out a finger and pointed to the house. "That bitch inside knows where my mate is, and by the time I'm done talking to her, she is going to spill her fucking guts, verbally or literally." Poppy stalked past the gaping men into the house.

If they got in her way, or tried one more time to treat her as delicate, she wouldn't be responsible for the bloodshed.

The study's door was closed, and slamming it open caused the woman tied to a chair to startle. Then Rosemary relaxed when she saw Poppy.

Poppy was pretty tired of people acting as if she was of no consequence, which was why she tipped the chair backward. Before it hit the floor, she straddled Rosemary's chest and leaned close.

"I'm going to ask some questions. If you choose not to answer, I will break something on your body. If you lie, I will know and snap a bone. Do we understand each other?"

Fear in the other woman's eyes didn't deter Poppy, not with Kit in danger. Besides, having lived through captivity at the hands of a sadistic man, she had no sympathy for anyone who enabled such behavior.

She tore the rag from the woman's mouth. "Where's Kit?"

"I don't—"

Poppy slammed Rosemary's head against the floor. "Let's try that again. Where is Kit?"

"At the golf club."

"Wrong. He was gone by the time we arrived."

Rosemary licked her lips. "I guess Teddy's plan to capture him for his boss worked."

"Where did your boyfriend take him?"

Rather than reply, Rosemary went off on a tangent. "Are you going to hurt Teddy? He was just following orders."

"Orders that hurt people. So, yes, he is going to get his stuffing yanked, no getting around that. You'll join him if you keep stalling. Who is his boss?"

"Boss. That's the only thing I've ever heard him called. He's supposedly super rich and has a thing for acquiring werewolves. Teddy says this is the second city where he's worked for him."

Second. Implying this had happened elsewhere, with others. Sickening, but she wasn't deterred.

"What does he want them for?"

A hesitation, before a deflated Rosemary whispered, "Hunting. According to Teddy, the boss and his buddies are big trophy hunters."

"Your boyfriend takes part in the killing of my people?"

Rosemary tried to shake her head. "No, that's not Teddy's thing. That's all the boss. He hosts special parties for his friends. The kind who can pay large."

"Where does this perversion occur?"

"I don't know." When Poppy would have

slapped her, Rosemary hurried to add, "I really don't. I was never invited, and Teddy only went once before we met, years and years ago. He couldn't show me pics since they're banned, but he told me about it. Says the place is creepy. The boss likes to mount his kills. Teddy says he had a couple of stuffed bears and deer, but mostly the boss is into wolves. Oh, and a few giant foxes."

The last piqued her interest. "What do you mean 'giant foxes'?"

She shrugged. "Maybe it's just the person stuffing them that's making them look bigger. All I know is Teddy said he ain't never seen such big ones. He's supposedly got a whole family on display, a vixen mother and a bunch of smaller pups."

It couldn't be... A coincidence surely, and yet, she couldn't help but recall Kit's odd parentage. Kit, who'd once been hunted.

Could it be the same man?

"What else can you tell me? I want to know everything."

Which turned out to be very little. In the previous city, Teddy had been given a list of names and told to collect those people and not get caught. It had taken him three years. This time, he'd had less to work with until the boss gave Teddy a custom-created wolf scent. Used as a perfume, it made their targets trust Rosemary and never suspect they were walking into a trap.

By the time Poppy ran out of questions, her stomach roiled and hopelessness assailed her. She rose from her crouched position over the woman, ignoring Darian, who'd kept silent for once as she got answers that didn't improve the situation. She was no closer to locating Kit and more worried about his well-being than ever.

As she moved away from Rosemary, the woman regained some of her cockiness. "Teddy won't let you get away with this. When he finds out what you did to me, he'll come after you."

Hammer entered the study, saying, "Doubtful." He held up his phone. Before Poppy could read the screen, he said, "Apparently, Theodore Kline suffered a heart attack while driving. Crashed his car into a building. He didn't survive."

There went her last hope of finding Kit.

Her chin lifted, and she howled. Frustrated and angry.

When her phone rang, her first impulse? Grab it and throw it against the wall. Hard.

It took restraint to instead glance at the screen.

Unknown number.

She answered. "Hello?"

"Is this Penelope?" the female voice on the other end asked.

"Who's asking?"

"Luna. I can't get a hold of Kit, and I'm worried."

She closed her eyes, and her chin dropped. "Kit's been taken by a hunter of Were."

"Then I guess we'd better get him back."

TWENTY-ONE

DISORIENTATION ASSAILED KIT AS HIS EYES opened—with effort, he should add. They felt heavy, as if weighted down with stones. He widened them far enough that he could see a blur, blinked to moisten them, and then opened them again.

He kind of wished his situation had stayed blurry. He closed his eyes, kept them shut tight, and took a few deep breaths. Fighting the panic. Hating the fear that nudged at the edges of his psyche.

He wouldn't let it take over. Couldn't, or he'd be lost. Now wasn't the time to lose focus or act rashly.

But it was hard to remind himself to be calm when he finally let himself look good and hard at the bars trapping him, one too small to stand or stretch his full length. He had his knees tucked to his chest.

A fucking cage.

No. Not again. The very thought had him freaking, his breathing coming in fast pants.

Calm. Fucking calm.

It was so damned hard, though.

I can't move.

He might be confined, but he had his wits. Ignoring the bars, he took stock of other things, starting with his nakedness.

The good news: He didn't feel any soreness from anal probing, needle sticking, or missing chunks. Such things hadn't happened to him before, but Kit had rescued a few Were caught by humans who'd experienced bad things.

The cinderblock walls and the single narrow window with bars over it indicated his prison was located in a basement. A prison he shared, he realized as he noted other cages with people inside.

Once he saw them, he couldn't look away. The terror on their faces chilled him. Their wan, hopeless expressions decimated his hope. Some stared back at him with wide eyes. A few slept. Still others, one a mere child, curled tight and shook as they silently cried.

He counted ten cages, only seven occupied. At last count, the decimated Pack had numbered more than seventeen.

Seventeen Were had gone missing, and not a

single one had been reported to the Lykosium. The situation might have passed unnoticed had he not gone looking for a pattern, the same one that had taken Penny's former Pack.

And his family.

How could this be happening? How could he have ended up a prisoner again of the man who'd killed everyone he cared about? Who'd almost killed Kit...

This time, the hunter could succeed. Kit could only hope he got a chance to fight back. If he could get loose before his muscles grew weak, he'd show the hunter who topped him in the food chain.

The stairs creaked as someone descended, reminding him of a time in the past when a different set of stairs had made similar noises.

This wouldn't be like last time. More prayer than fact. But the small child had grown into a man. A strong man. He could fight.

If he could escape the cage.

The footsteps approached from behind. He had just enough room that he could have turned to see, but that action would show interest. *Never draw attention.* The rule his mother had taught, because that was all she could do when the hunter had caught the family.

The first time, she'd surrendered so that her

young kits might survive awhile longer. But they had been young, so the hunter had imprisoned them in a room, waiting for them to grow so they could offer actual sport.

He still had nightmares about that basement room, with the ragged blankets, the metal bowls, and the bucket they'd had to piss and shit in.

His home for... He never did find out how long, because back then he'd had no sense of time. His recollections of those desperate days were a blur of his mother as she'd tried to teach her kits how to survive. As they'd grown stronger, and smarter, they'd fashioned an escape plan. They'd gotten out of that prison room, leaving their caretaker in a pool of blood and spilled dog food. They'd made it to the woods before the hunter had noticed.

The baying of the hounds had provided their first warning. The thunder of many hooves had revealed that their captor didn't track alone.

Mother had died trying to protect Kit and the others. A valiant vixen, she hadn't been able to prevail against four grown men armed with guns and sharp spears. In defense of her, Kit had gotten hurt. They all had. But the hunter had healed them, only so he could release them for sport and kill them one by one.

The man responsible stood in front of his cage, smirking.

"I always hoped one day we'd meet again, Tristan."

The name hit him hard. Because it was the name his mother gave him. Forgotten during the trauma. And that name would stay dead, because Tristan ceased to exist the day his mother died.

He said nothing.

"Silent treatment? I see you haven't changed. Only your brother never shut up. What was his name again? Ronny? Roddy?"

Kit closed his eyes as the name came to him. Robert.

"Do you know how you ended up in my custody all those years ago?"

He wanted to say he didn't care, and yet, he listened avidly.

"Blame your father. He was hunting in my woods. Poaching my game when I caught him. Imagine my surprise when he shifted into a man."

"He broke the code."

"He didn't just spill your Were secret, he smashed it to bits. Told me everything to save his skin. Even the fact he was married and had a bunch of kids. Were beasts, just like him."

It killed him to know the father he didn't

remember had been too cowardly to keep them safe. Kit would die before revealing any secrets.

"Your mother almost slipped my trap. If she'd made it to the creek that day, I probably would have lost your trail. But luck was on my side, and I caught you all."

"You'll pay for this." Perhaps not by Kit's hand, but someone would kill this monster. Luna, most likely. By now, she'd tracked him and was plotting his rescue. Or so he hoped. She'd better move quickly. He didn't get the impression the hunter would wait long.

"You've grown quite big since we last saw each other. You were, what, five, six, when you escaped?"

"Too old to remember?" he taunted.

"The ladies call me distinguished." The man had matured, his hair more grayish-white than dark, but he was annoyingly attractive in spite of it.

"Are you sure that's not praise for your money?"

"Can't it be both?"

"I see you're still a sadistic fucker."

"Everyone needs a hobby."

The man's cheerfulness grated on him. He was just as slick as before, maybe even more so.

"You won't get away with this."

"I already have. Don't tell me you're expecting rescue. Hate to tell you, Tristan, but they'll never be able to locate you. We've already disabled the chips in your body. I must admit the technology is kind of ingenious and something I'll be more watchful for in the next batch we recruit."

"There will be no more of your sadistic games," Kit spat.

"On that, you're wrong. We both know there's plenty more wolves out there. Not foxes, though. It appears your little family was a rarity. I will say, if I'd thought for an instant you'd survive to adulthood, I wouldn't have sterilized you. You'd have made an interesting stud."

There went his assumption that he'd been born incapable of impregnating a woman. Kit almost gagged to realize how he'd been robbed.

"It is my sincere hope you die painfully," he said through gritted teeth.

"You know, you wouldn't be the first to try to kill me. I've been shot, had my house set on fire. My own girlfriend even tried to kill me once." The hunter practically giggled.

"Must be because you're such a nice guy."

"I am. To humans. But animals are good for only one thing. Take a guess what that thing is." The hunter leaned close to the bars. "Providing for humans. Because we are the dominant species."

"Does that thought help you sleep at night?" Kit

taunted, unable to help himself. Maybe he'd die quickly, or the hunter would want to challenge him sooner than later.

"Speaking of night time activities, that girlfriend of yours is attractive. Don't know why she's wasting herself on a man who can't fill her belly with a child."

His heart almost stopped. "Stay away from Penny!"

"You're the one who should stay away. Does she know you'll never give her little firecrackers? Maybe someone should tell her."

Not responding to the cruel taunt almost killed him. *Don't react.* Showing he cared would just encourage the hunter to go after her.

He managed to remain impassive until the hunter said, "I'm not too old to seed the next generation. How about I help you out with the impregnation part? Maybe I'll even let you watch."

Kit roared, incoherent with terrified rage.

The hunter laughed. "Howl all you want. It's going to happen. And soon. The tip about your whereabouts I planted has ensured she's already on her way."

Penny was coming to try to save him? That humbled and hardened his resolve. He wrapped himself in the knowledge that she wouldn't come alone. She'd have Darian at the very least.

Yet, while he wanted rescue, he also prayed she'd turn around and go home.

Because when the dying started, he didn't want her anywhere close.

TWENTY-TWO

"How much longer until we get there?" Poppy complained. The whining grated on her own last nerve. However, she couldn't help herself as the anxiety mounted.

They'd embarked on this last leg of the trip after a long flight that had taken them across the country and over a border. Luna met them at the airport, looking frazzled and yet still attractive with her silvery striped hair. But her eyes? Those unnerved Poppy. The woman had an otherness to her that she'd never encountered. Were all those on the council strange like her?

They rented an oversized SUV and headed for a location Luna refused to divulge, insisting on doing the driving herself.

"We're not far now," was Luna's reply.

The non-answer did little to dispel Poppy's unease, especially as the highway signs became familiar.

Her nails dug into her palms. *Please let me be wrong.* She'd hoped to never return. Never—

They exited the highway, and the dread hit her hard, because she recognized this area. Knew every twist and turn in the road they traveled. After all, she'd escaped on it years ago with Darian's aid.

"Where are you taking us?" she whispered.

"I think you know our final destination," Luna calmly said, confirming Poppy's fear.

The SUV turned onto a rutted path in the woods, the twin beams of the headlights bouncing off the foliage. They'd left the road well before reaching the tree-lined driveway that led up to the house.

The house that had burned down.

"Why would he come here? There's nothing to see. A fire took the place to the ground."

"It was rebuilt last year," Luna stated as she placed the vehicle in park, the woods pressing in on all sides.

The implication shook Poppy. It couldn't be. She asked softly, "Is it Gerard?"

Had he escaped the burning house? Could it be possible she and Kit shared a common past and enemy?

It chilled her to the depths of her soul to realize she'd come full circle. Her past had caught up to her present.

"I never knew the name of Kit's captor," Luna said. In her recounting of past events, she always called him *that hunter*, sometimes adding *fucker* or *bastard*.

Darian opened the car door and offered a gruff, "If it is Gerard, we'll take care of him, once and for all."

A bitter part of Poppy almost said, *Like last time?* Gerard still hurt people because he kept escaping the jaws of death.

Luna had failed. Her mother. Darian too. Knowing Kit, he'd try his damnedest. What hope did they have against a human who seemed to have more lives than a cat?

Don't you dare turn coward now. She dropped her chin and took a deep breath. Steady. She could do this.

Had to.

Because not acting wasn't an option.

She eyed the woods, blinking as the SUV's headlights shut off. Her vision adjusted as she remembered her panicked run through the woods. She'd relived it in so many nightmares that now she could glance around and actually remain calm. It wasn't so scary right now, despite the darkness.

I survived once. I can do it again. After all, she was older, stronger, and she hadn't come alone.

"We going in on two or four?" she asked, hoping no one noticed she was barely keeping her shit together.

"I'm not sure what we should expect in terms of resistance," Luna admitted. "Given how stretched we are, I'm afraid there was no real time to study the place."

"Meaning we have no idea how many people to expect," Lochlan grumbled. "I'll assume they're armed."

"Most likely."

Poppy bit her lip. She almost apologized for asking them to help her rescue Kit. Then again, she knew that even if she'd told them to leave, they wouldn't. Kit was one of them. He'd risk his life to save them. They wouldn't do any less.

Hammer pointed. "I smell gun oil. That way." Given he had the best olfactory sense of them all, she didn't doubt his statement.

"Guess that answers one question. And me without a Kevlar vest," Lochlan drawled. "Fantastic."

"Want to stay behind?" Luna taunted.

"Like fuck. Been a while since I've been challenged."

"You didn't sound happy."

Hammer snorted. "FYI, that was Loch's happy face."

True fact. Poppy eyed the older man, who of them all had the most experience in this kind of situation, except maybe for Luna. But she trusted Lochlan.

"What should we do?"

"Not go in as a nattering bunch," Lochlan said. "The boys will go in fur. Triangle formation. The ladies will head for the house."

Luna uttered a very unladylike sound. "Well, fuck, aren't you just a peach telling us little ladies what to do?"

"You have a different idea?" Lochlan asked with an arched brow.

Apparently, Darian did. "We could drive the SUV right in. Maybe if we all confront this asshole together, he'll hand over Kit to save his skin."

"Because a guy who loves to hunt our kind is going to roll over and give us what we want?" Poppy couldn't stem the sarcasm at her brother's ill-thought idea.

"See what I told you? Mating made her mean," Darian moaned to Hammer.

"About time that girl found her spine," Lochlan muttered.

"She's a woman, not a girl," Luna sassed. "I see sexism is alive and well in your world."

"Since you have a problem with it, would you prefer to go in on four legs, then?" Lochlan asked. "I'd be glad to keep my fucking pants on for once."

They shared a glare.

Before the disagreement devolved, Poppy jumped in. "The plan is fine, Lochlan. Luna and I will go in on two feet." On another day, she would have sided with Luna and blasted them for sexism with gendered role appropriation, but quite honestly, she didn't want to be in her fur when she met the man who'd taken Kit. She wanted to give him a piece of her mind. And then a few punches to the face. Then she'd kill him. Because she knew better than to waste a good revenge. In the movies, those that hesitated usually suffered an avoidable tragedy. It was why a zombie should always be double tapped.

They ditched the car, and the men shed and stuffed their clothes into a pair of knapsacks that Luna and Poppy carried. They both wore loose clothing with shoes they could easily slip off. Poppy had even eschewed a bra or panties. She'd once seen a friend get caught in her knickers during a shift.

Nothing more ridiculous looking than a wolf wearing a thong.

Poppy and Luna didn't say much. They'd done their talking on the trip.

"So you're the one who saved and adopted Kit," had been Poppy's opening line.

To which Luna had stared at her and gasped, "Holy fuck, you're mated."

The good news was they got along decently. The bad was Luna told her about Kit's rescue. How he was the last alive of his family. How he'd lived in a cage. How he'd suffered through torture.

It broke her damned heart.

"We can't let that man keep him."

"The reign of terror on our kind ends today," Luna promised.

But would it put a stop to Poppy's nightmares?

Poppy hadn't been in these woods for a few years, but she recognized landmarks. After all, she'd run through them more than a few times during her visits to her mom before she'd become Gerard's prisoner.

How had she not known the house had been rebuilt? Could it truly be Gerard? She wouldn't doubt he'd have the balls to put a new house atop the ashes of the old. After all, who returned to the scene of their crimes? Murdering psychos who tortured children, that's who.

As they neared the house, Poppy quieted her steps and paid attention to where she placed her feet. The trio of wolves remained out of sight, but she knew they watched.

Their presence reassured her. So did the gun tucked at her back. She'd taken Rosemary's weapon despite Darian's objections of *no guns.*

Her reply: *Everyone knows you don't bring claws to a gunfight.* It should be printed on a T-shirt.

Luckily, Lochlan had agreed. She hadn't asked how he'd managed to smuggle his gun onto their flight given Canada had strict laws. All she knew was it would protect them if she needed it to, because she'd learned how to shoot just over a year ago. Lochlan, the father she'd never had, taught her.

The edge of the forest provided a hidden spot to observe the house. The new building, a log house, featured big trunks that crisscrossed at the corners. The front porch loomed more than twelve feet high. A guy with a rifle across his chest guarded it.

A quiet peek left and right showed two more guards in tree houses at the edges of the cleared woods. Four spots would have been smarter. They'd left a few holes in their surveillance.

Luna tapped Poppy's arm and pointed to the threats she'd already noted.

The wolves remained out of sight.

Luna tilted a finger at the house. Floodlights all around kept it well lit, but they were currently on a low setting, providing just enough light to show movement on the tended grass around the place. They'd need a distraction to get across undetected.

Just then, a yell was cut off. As the guard across from the one who'd yelled climbed down from his perch, Poppy sprinted, moving quickly toward the west wall.

Luna shadowed a few paces behind. A rifle went off with a crack. Unfortunate, because that would bring attention they couldn't afford.

Suddenly, the hard surface beneath Poppy's feet collapsed. A pit opened up, and for a moment, it seemed that Poppy ran on air. Then gravity grabbed and yanked her down.

TWENTY-THREE

FALLING DIDN'T LAST LONG. POPPY HIT THE spongy bottom hard.

Oomph.

It took a few blinks and breaths to collect her wits. The faint moonlight barely penetrated the darkness at the bottom of the pit. *Please let there not be anything that scuttles with too many legs.* Watching *Indiana Jones and the Temple of Doom* had traumatized her for life.

Luna peeked over the edge. "Penelope?"

She groaned and sat up. "Down here. Nothing broken, I think."

"I'll get you out. Hang tight."

As if she could go anywhere.

She paced the pit, eyeing the walls for hand-holds. She felt so dumb. She'd not scented or sensed anything amiss and literally run into the trap.

The dirt walls didn't offer much to hold on to, but she still tried to scale the sides. The width proved just enough to foil all attempts. Dirt crumbled and dumped her back down to the bottom.

A heavy sigh escaped her. Trapped. She would surely be discovered any second now.

A rustle overhead had her really hoping for Luna or one of the guys with some rope.

A glance up showed an unwelcome visage, though. Her nightmare come true.

Gerard.

Even though she'd expected it, the sight of his smarmy smile hit her hard.

"Penelope, how delightful of you to drop in. So nice to see you."

"I can't say the same," she snapped, rather than give in to the gut-wrenching fear.

"Aren't you the feisty one? I'd forgotten the resemblance to your mother. Attractive woman. Shame about her dying."

"You killed her."

"Like I said, a shame. She had excellent genes and birthing hips. If she'd not died, I was planning to impregnate her until we got it right. I guess with her gone, you'll do."

"I'm barren because of you, asshole."

"Well, that's a fucking shame. Oh well. I'm sure you'll have other uses. After all, you are passably attractive, and I have needs."

Her stomach churned. "Over my dead body."

"How about willing, because wouldn't you know? I have something for that."

She almost puked. "No. I won't let you."

"Let?" He laughed. "Once I dose you, you'll be floating on a cloud and won't say a word when I'm sticking my dick in you."

"Coward. Is that the only way you can get some, by drugging a woman?"

"Actually, seeing your despondency when you wake up and realize what I've done will be an added thrill."

This level of evil just didn't seem possible. "You're sick."

"You just refuse to acknowledge that I am better than your kind. More alpha than the most alpha."

At that, she laughed. "You don't have anywhere close to the awe and presence of a true Alpha. You're pathetic."

"Says the loser to the winner." A rope dropped into the pit. "Be a good girl and climb."

"Make me." While it was hard to sound brave, she tried to goad him into doing something reckless.

"As if I'd be so stupid. I'll wait for the sedative to take effect."

Panic filled her. If he drugged her, she couldn't fight him. "You won't get away with this."

"I already have. See, I've captured all your friends. That old woman? Being chained up as we speak. Your brother and his stocky friend? Already in cages."

She didn't react when he missed listing one of her companions. If Lochlan remained free, they had a chance.

"There's a special place in Hell for someone like you," she said as he tossed something down that exploded into a drifting powder she couldn't avoid breathing in.

"It's called by the right hand of the devil. Good night, Penelope. Have a good sleep. You'll need it."

Ominous words to hear before she fell asleep and woke to a nightmare.

TWENTY-FOUR

KIT MANAGED TO DOZE AND DREAMED…

He slept in a cage, alone. The last of his siblings had disappeared a while ago, and he was the only one left in the basement. The hunter—"call me master" —had fitted a metal collar around his neck so he could exercise for a short time each day.

Given no one remained to supervise, he usually scrabbled around, testing the limits of his leash. A few times, he tried to break free by sprinting, only to have the collar choke him as the chain went taut.

Food came once a day in a bowl with a bottle of water. Only meat because, as the hunter stated, "People don't pay me to hunt a fat fox bastard."

He didn't know what the word bastard *meant, but he assumed it was bad. At times, he wondered what he'd done to deserve this punishment. He used to miss life from before, but when all he remembered was hurt, he decided to forget, to block all things that made him cry. Such as his mother. He couldn't even remember her face anymore.*

Nor his name.

This was his world, and when the hunter came for him one day and said, "It's time," he felt such relief.

"Wake up. It's time." Someone rattled the bars of his cage, waking him from his light sleep.

"Geezus, where the fuck did the boss find a ginger? I didn't think his kind came in anything but shades of brown and black."

"I heard he's a freak of nature. Part fox, part wolf," the guard smelling of spearmint said in a low voice.

The one reeking of tobacco snorted. "His daddy got a little moonstruck and put his dick in the wrong doggy?"

That almost had Kit reacting. In truth, he didn't know how he'd come into being. Fox shifters weren't supposed to exist. And though Luna had looked—Kit too, as he'd gotten older—they'd never found any others. The Kitsune legends didn't seem to apply to his very Caucasian ass.

The guards gripped the bars of his prison on either end and hoisted. Being relocated from the basement didn't bode well.

Guess it's my turn to be tortured.

The question was, could the prey turn on the hunter?

The guards paid no mind to those staring as they carted Kit past. None of the prisoners uttered a sound, but their sullen expressions indicated they didn't expect him to return. He didn't either. If this was like his last stay with the hunter, once you left the basement, you died.

I've survived before, though. Kit had been the only one to break free. Could he be lucky a third time? If he got a chance to fight, he might change the odds.

Unfortunately, they'd not fed him since his capture. No hydration either. The good news? He'd gotten sharper as time passed, the drugs in his system wearing off. So he was aware of everything, including the identities of the new prisoners who'd been brought to the basement—Luna, Darian, and Hammer, the latter barely fitting in his cage with those stocky shoulders.

Last of all had been Lochlan, who snored louder than the rest.

All drugged. Victims of an ambush they'd never suspected.

Only one person didn't appear.

The one Kit most needed to see. *Where are you, Penny?*

As the guards went up the stairs, his cage tilted so that his head hung down. The top of his skull pressed against bars made of lightweight metal that was still too strong for him to bend. The men hit the main floor of the house and moved through the kitchen, its massive counter bare of food, and into a two-story great room hosting a party in full swing. That was where Kit found his mate. With unerring accuracy, his veered to his Penny, dressed in white, head lolling, eyes closed. Drugged and asleep in the chair she'd been deposited in.

No. He bristled, raged, and inwardly cried a little. Had she been hurt? This was his fault.

The wallowing in guilt lasted only a moment. So long as he lived, there was still a chance. But only if he reined in his emotions and paid attention.

The party attendees, all men, wore combat pants and camo shirts. Ten in total. Loud and brash, some gripping bottles of beer, others with club glasses that held alcohol on the rocks. He flashed back to the last time he'd been a captive of the hunter, when he'd been not even a third of his current size. He'd felt terror as the strange men had poked at him and passed his leash around.

This time, they could only look, their faces

different than the ones he recalled but their words and excitement familiar. All eager for the hunt.

Guess who they'd be chasing?

A utensil rapped against a glass as a man called for their attention. "Shut up for a second. I want to make a speech."

"Zip it, Lemongrass."

"Do you have to?" someone else griped.

Lemongrass tilted his double chins. "Yeah, I do, Potvin, because I want to thank our host for this amazing opportunity. I've never had a chance to hunt a shapeshifter before, but my dad did. He loved it. Called it the ultimate rush. And now today, I'll get to understand why he loved hunting them so much. So, thank you, Gerard."

"My pleasure." Gerard, looking slick and pompous in his camouflage regalia, smoothly accepted the praise.

"A toast to killing the monsters that dare to live amongst us!" yelled Potvin, his florid cheeks not a sign of great health.

"And to our host, Gerard, for making this possible." Lemongrass held up his glass. "Cheers."

Gerard didn't drink, though, his rapier gaze falling on everyone and everything except Kit. As if he didn't matter.

A power play, which had terrified him as a child,

but as a man, he saw right through it. Gerard could ooze all the confidence he wanted, this fox and pony show was about combatting his inferiority. At the very root of the hunter, he feared. They all did.

Take the leader out and, most likely, the others would crumble.

As the men guzzled their booze and buzzed with excitement, Kit stared at Penny. Trying to will her to move. Drugs didn't work the same on Were as humans. But Gerard, the same man who'd once tortured his Penny, would know how to dose someone with their metabolism.

Key example: Kit, awake for the show.

"How is your, uh, specimen gonna shapeshift if there's no full moon?" a puny, nervous fellow asked, shoving his glasses higher on his nose.

"I'm glad you asked." Gerard smiled. "Turns out werewolves—or as they like to call themselves, the Were—have been around a long time. So long, in fact, our ancestors developed ways to deal with them. Some of those ways have been lost because, after we almost wiped them out, the knowledge fell to the wayside. But through extensive research, I located bits and pieces of those ways. I learned how to replicate their scent to lure them out. Even figured out how to hide my own scent. Nothing funnier than dousing yourself in anti-scent and sneaking up on one." Gerard shared a sly, conspiratorial smile. "My pride and joy, though, is the powder you're about to see in action. Watch closely, gentlemen."

All gazes turned on Gerard as he neared Kit's cage, a smirk on his lips. He crouched. "Lucky fox. I'm going to let you out. And then I'll even count to ten to give you a running head start before I let these eager boys come after you."

Kit's lip curled. "Fuck running. I'll kill you."

"So predictable and wrong. You'll run. You won't be able to help yourself, because you won't be yourself. An interesting side effect, as the drug brings out the primal in your kind. And I just want you to know that while you're racing for your life, I'm going to be here plowing your girlfriend, even though she's barren, because I know the thought will drive you mental."

On that, Gerard was correct. Kit trembled with rage. "You'll die. Slowly. Painfully."

"And those, gentlemen, are his final words." Gerard stood, his hand outstretched to empty a bag.

The innocuous-appearing sifting powder couldn't be avoided. It got on his skin. On his lashes. On his lips. Up his nose. The finely ground dust sank into his flesh.

At first, it tickled, easily ignored in favor of watching Gerard. The creak of metal followed the slotting and turning of the key in the padlock on his cage. Kit readied to pounce.

His flesh began to itch where the powder had settled. Annoying. Also ignored.

The door to his prison swung open, and Kit shoved himself forward, only to fall as a burning sensation ripped through him.

Before he started screaming, he heard Gerard say, "Gentlemen, who's ready to hunt?"

TWENTY-FIVE

THE POUNDING IN LUNA'S HEAD WASN'T JUST because of the sleeping drug but also from shame, because she'd failed.

Not only had she not managed to rescue Kit—thus breaking her promise to always protect him—she'd also never made it back to Penelope. She'd gravely miscalculated and led them all into a trap.

Her fault. For a while, she'd suspected that something reeked within the Lykosium, but she hadn't pursued it because she couldn't figure out where the rot originated. But when Penelope had fallen into that hole in the ground, indicating preparation on the part of the hunter, Luna realized they'd been set up.

She'd never made it to the woods. Men without scents had stepped from behind bushes, aiming tranquilizer guns. They'd fired before she could call out a warning.

Betrayed, because the formula to mask scent was a closely guarded Lykosium secret.

Tranquilized like an animal, Luna had awakened a prisoner. Unlike most of the others who'd been captured, Luna hadn't ended up in a cage, because, apparently, they'd run out. Ten cages, ten captives, including her recent companions. She scented Darian and Hammer, Kit too. Plus one more, also in chains, but she chose to ignore him for now.

No sign of Penelope, though. That didn't bode well, because despite the drugs, she vaguely recalled a male voice stating, *"She's too old to be any use for breeding. I learned that with the last over-the-hill bitch I tried."*

Rude. She had plenty of good birthing years left. Okay, maybe one. None. Fuck him. Luna had been busy trying to serve and save the Were. Besides, she'd raised a wonderful son in Kit.

A boy she'd failed, given the source of his night-mares had returned. In her defense, she'd tried to find the person who'd caught and tortured Kit and his family. She'd tried to locate the person who rented the lodge, to no avail. Records showed it being leased by a shell company and used by a great many of its employees.

Busy with a child and her duties as enforcer, she'd not dug as deep as she should have. A mistake given current circumstance. Fucking past came back to bite her.

By her side, a grizzled male began to stir. Lochlan of the Feral Pack. Previous origin unknown, before he ended up in Northern Alberta. Odd, and not a priority right now. Escaping was.

The chains around her wrists and ankles rattled as she moved. Snug to the skin and embedded in the wall, the chains were welded shut and too thick to break. But at least she wasn't prone in a cage. Her heart ached and her anger seethed to see her kind treated so terribly.

Lochan's eyes opened, and he regarded her flatly. "I don't suppose you have a hacksaw."

The dry query surprised her. "No."

"Me either." He glanced down at his naked body. A fine body. "I hate it when they chain you up."

She tried to not blink at the reply. Interesting fellow. She might have to look deeper into this man once they got out of here.

If they got out of here. Things didn't look too good at the moment.

Lochlan pulled forward on his chains, the length too short for him to fully extend his arms.

"They're set in cement," she mentioned.

"Of course they are." He leaned forward and grunted as he flexed. The big man somehow got bigger, his muscles, the cords in his neck, and the veins in his arms all bulging.

Pop. The chain on his left side snapped.

The right took less effort, given he could wrap his free hand around it. He heaved with a ripple of exertion, and his efforts paid off, as he freed his other arm. The dangling chains jingled as Lochlan flexed and stretched.

"Impressive," she commented, and she didn't just mean his strength. The man had a fine physique and an interesting trail of silver fur down his chest.

"Not really. More like too many swings of an ax to stock the woodpile." He played down the feat that not many could have claimed. "Time for the legs."

His knees were already bent to accommodate the short chains. He grabbed one ankle tether and snapped it then the next. Unleashed, he stood and stretched, looming over her, a truly large man, handsome, too, if you liked them rugged—and she did. Something Luna hadn't thought about in years. Hard to not think of sex with his dick hanging out and his washboard stomach tempting.

Would he like it soft and gentle or rough and sweaty?

Now wasn't the time to suddenly remember she might be in her fifties but she was still a woman. Luna held out her wrists. "If you don't mind."

"I'm thinking maybe I shouldn't, given you seem to attract trouble."

"How do you figure that?" was her sour reply.

"This place needed more than a handful of us attacking."

"We weren't supposed to attack but retrieve," she grumbled. She wasn't about to admit she'd underestimated their foe because of seriously lacking intel. Or had someone intentionally left out important information in hopes of luring her here?

Lochlan glanced around the basement and all the cages holding people. *Their* people, even if many were strangers. "This fucker has quite the enterprise going. How the hell has he evaded notice for so long?" He placed an accusing stare on her.

She wanted to offer a hot retort to his criticism, but he had a point. This kind of thing shouldn't have been possible. The Lykosium existed to prevent this. Yet, if it weren't for Kit's investigating, they'd never have known.

The possibility of a traitor on the council, one who'd been hiding this maniac's actions, left a sour taste in her mouth.

"You're not the only one wondering how this

happened. But can we save the accusations for later?" She held up her wrists. "Set me free so we can do something about it."

"Still not convinced that's a good idea."

"Consider it an order from the Lykosium."

"Didn't take you for the type to pull rank." He crouched and grabbed a chain to her right.

"I didn't take you for the chatty type."

He grunted and yanked. *Snap. Snap.* Wrists then ankles. He freed her and drawled, "Now what, oh mighty council member?"

"Get everyone out of the cages and ready to bolt. I'll scout for a way out."

At her suggestion, he snorted. "How about I spy, and you play rescuing hero?"

She eyed him. "A six-foot-something naked man might be a little more noticeable than me."

Again, he made a derisive sound. "As if you'd blend in any better with those eyes and attitude."

"What's that supposed to mean? You have a problem with assertive women?"

"I have a problem when you drag people into situations without being properly prepared."

"And what would you have done differently?"

"I would have ditched the car much earlier. Come in on foot with guns. I'd have set up a sniper position in a tree and sent in someone to draw the guards out."

"Spoken by a former military man."

"By a still-living military man. You, as a former enforcer, should have known better than to come in without backup."

"You and the others were supposed to provide it."

He stared at her. "Seriously? Three untrained civilians—one of them suffering PTSD and mated to the target we're here to rescue—is your idea of backup? This operation should have merited a full enforcer squad."

"None were available," she mumbled.

"What do you mean 'none were available'? What the fuck are they doing that's more important?"

"First off, we don't have as many as you think working for us. Not anymore. Their numbers have been dwindling the last few years." Attrition, accidents. In the past, it would have been a big deal, but most issues these days could be handled electronically. Much of what they did consisted of erasing video evidence, tweets, and blogs and, when that didn't work, discrediting the poster.

"You had enough to send a team after Samuel when he came after Rok and Meadow at the ranch."

"I did." Then more softly, "That team, with the

exception of Kit, has since gone missing." Now probably wasn't a good time to admit that. "They were last seen in this area."

"Fucking hell, lady, are you shitting me?" Lochlan glared. "And you just thought to mention this now?"

"I didn't know who I could trust."

"So instead, you trusted no one and fucked us all."

"I did what I thought best." She tried to temper her irritation. They needed to move quickly if they were going to rescue Kit. She could smell him in this room. He'd been here, an empty spot among the cages an ominous sign.

While Lochlan took off to check out the lay of the land, she moved among the imprisoned. They clung to the bars of their cages and offered soft pleas as she eyeballed the padlocks. She'd need something to open them. A toolbox provided a screwdriver that she used to wedge into the locks and twist them apart.

A few inhabitants didn't immediately react to their freedom. Others slid from their cages quietly and huddled on the floor, uncertain. Only one, an enforcer she recognized and had thought lost, nodded and murmured, "Thanks."

She had no reply, because they'd obviously taken

too long to come to the rescue, given Harry was the only one left of his squad. He grabbed a tool to help her with the rest of the cages, and soon, with two more helpers, everyone was free.

Slowly, the survivors gathered in a group at Luna's back, which was when Lochlan joined them to report his findings. Despite the fact he remained nude, he appeared at home among the others. Luna was the one to feel conspicuous in her clothes.

"We'll have to go up the stairs and through the house."

"That doesn't sound ideal," she stated.

"It's the only way out. Most won't fit through the windows even if we could get the bars off. Not to mention, we'd be sitting ducks as we emerged."

Luna eyed the stairs and grimaced. "Frontal assault it is."

"We'll shift. It will make us faster," suggested one of the former captives.

"Excellent idea. Those who feel strong enough, take the lead, maybe buddy up with someone who's struggling." She made it a suggestion, knowing no Were would be left behind.

"If we go on four legs, what about doors?" someone asked.

"I'll stay as is to handle anything that requires fingers." Too much shifting, and those she'd released would start collapsing. The body could do only so much.

"Everyone ready?" Lochlan asked. His air of competence proved contagious. A few more spines straightened. "Once we get to the main floor, head for the closest exit and get to the woods. Expect resistance. Try to get past it if you can. A mile south of here, you'll find a car with some gear."

A few of the bodies shifted.

"Run away?" someone muttered.

"It's called staying alive," was Luna's reply.

"For how long if that fucker is left to keep hunting us?" snapped a woman with bruises that hurt Luna on a personal level.

"What if we want to fight?" Harry offered.

"I don't know how many we'd be up against. I don't need to tell you they're armed. Dangerous. Deadly."

"So are we." The tiniest of them, a teenage girl, stepped forward. "This time, I won't hesitate to kill."

"Killing bites or nothing," said another.

"Have to stop them."

More murmurs arose.

Luna glanced over the group of gaunt faces. These people were dirty and scared. But also brave and determined. And aware that this wasn't a threat they could walk away from.

There was only one thing she could say. "May the moon shine brightly upon your vengeance this night," she quoted, not remembering the author, or even the exact words, but loving the sentiment.

"Fight. Fight." The soft chant raised bumps on her skin, and the very air shivered as they all began to shift. With that change, some of their swagger returned.

Luna fed it. "You are Were. There are none more powerful than us. None stronger. Faster. Smarter." Her voice softened. "And when one is threatened..."

Lochlan, the last one standing, looked her in the eye as he said, "We take them out." He shifted right after those words into a large specimen of silver and deep gray. Beautiful. She kept her hands to herself, though. Petting was intimate and shouldn't be done casually.

He alone padded by her side as she climbed the steps. Wincing at each creak. Eyeing the door and hoping it wouldn't suddenly get peppered with bullets. She made it to the top landing. She put her hand on the knob and turned it.

It opened onto a guard with his gun lowered. "Hands up," he began to say, only his eyes widened when he saw who slipped past her. The gun dipped as Lochlan dove for the ankles, and it was a good thing he hit them hard. A shot sailed harmlessly over his head. The soldier went down. It took very little to ensure he'd never get up again, and he kindly died without getting out a warning.

Relief filled her. They now had a chance.

She glanced back at the stairs filled with wolves and said, "Move out."

A furry tide flowed into the kitchen, splitting off in pairs, Harry and his partner heading for the stairs, the rest toward the door to the outside. The kitchen island hid most of their activity, not that there appeared to be anyone in sight. Luna remained tucked by the cabinets and did her best not to flinch at the bugling of a horn.

The hunt began. A hunt for her son, Kit. As the last of the wolves fled, she stepped into the open, Lochlan by her side, ready to join the others. But then she noticed someone in the far corner of the massive great room across from the kitchen. As she stepped closer, she briefly glanced around the two-story space decorated with mounted animal heads. Then she saw the unconscious Penelope, and standing over her the man Luna should have tried harder to kill so long ago.

To distract him, she drawled, "You must be Gerard. I don't think we've met."

He whirled, arching a brow in surprise. "If it isn't the old bitch from the basement."

"You made a grave mistake in coming after my people," she stated as she moved fully into the room, aware without looking that Lochlan flanked her on the left. She kept Gerard focused on her. "I expected someone more impressive."

He laughed. "Do you think I'm going to suddenly go into a rage and do something stupid that will get me killed while you're poorly insulting me?" His rapier gaze mocked that assumption. "I've been killing your kind for thirty years. It started with Tristan's family, as a matter of fact. I caught a wolf in a trap, only lo and behold, he wasn't just a wolf. Imagine my delight when he told me about his fox wife and kids to save his life."

She could have gagged. "You killed those children."

"Children. Mothers. Fathers. I try to not discriminate." His wide smile sickened.

"Why?" she whispered.

"Because I can."

The reply of a monster with no conscience. "Someone's been helping you." She stated that as fact. After he'd killed the fox family, he'd obviously found others somehow.

He confirmed. "Indeed, someone has. The very man who betrayed his son. Did you know he now serves on your precious council? How does it feel to know someone close has betrayed you?"

His turn to try to distract. She hardened her disappointment in her kind. The man who had betrayed them would pay with his life. After she handled this monster. "Who is the father?" She'd never been able to find out.

"Don't tell me the mighty council member doesn't know," he mocked, still unafraid. He had a hand in his pocket. Grabbing for a weapon?

"Awfully cocky for a man in a room with several Were," she remarked. Did he have a gun? They could easily handle a knife.

"I know how to control your kind." He withdrew his hand, which held a small drawstring bag.

The leather of the sack blocked its scent. "Is that all you've got?" she taunted.

"It's all I—"

Lochlan lunged, a leap that should have worked, but Gerard proved prepared. With his other hand, he flung a powder into Lochlan' face, the same sleeping shit that had taken her out earlier.

The big wolf hit the floor, groggy, not fully out but useless for the moment.

Holding her breath, Luna sprinted for Gerard, who turned in time to dump the contents of the leather bag. The powder hung in the air as she passed through it. She didn't mean to breathe it in, but a tickle seized her throat, and she gasped. It filled her, a burning dust that entered her lungs then her veins.

She screamed.

And screamed and screamed, because it hurt as the beast she usually kept locked away tore its way out.

TWENTY-SIX

A fuzzy cloud filled Poppy's head until she heard the scream, a never-ending wail of agony that ended in a terrifying howl.

She wrenched her eyes open to a nightmare. The monster, a thing of slavering teeth and massive claws, had a ridged back and whipping tail. A wolf, but not the kind she'd ever encountered.

Poppy would have screamed if she hadn't feared taking a breath would draw its terrible gaze. Instead, an instinct for flight kicked her into running for the garden doors. The handle gave at her twist and push, releasing her into the night air. She glanced up and saw dawn ready to crest. A horn in the distance announced the call to the hunt.

In the distance, she saw men riding out on horses, racing after the hounds that bayed their excitement as they chased a flash of red heading into the woods.

Red.

Red?

Fox.

Kit.

Her sluggish mind made the connection, and so she ran after them, too, her legs tangling in the gown she couldn't remember putting on. Stupid thing got in her way.

Then it didn't. She raced on four sure feet, senses sharper, the drug wearing off at the edges. Behind her, she heard a surprised scream and the sound of shots fired.

I hope Gerard is the one shot. For a second, she stumbled and halted. She veered around to glance in the direction of the house. She'd run away to escape a wolf monster, only to leave behind a human monster. She had to ensure Gerard died.

The barking of hounds drew her attention. She glanced in the direction where Kit fled. He was more important.

She raced, leaping over ruts and branches. She stumbled only when a sharp yelp was followed by silence. Then howls erupted, a few snarls and a scream of rage that raised her hackles.

The ululation that came next was maddened by

pain. But recognizable. Her mate hurt. She had to find him.

She sprinted through the woods, seeking. The next cry came from a dying human, and it lingered long enough that she heard the panic in the erratic pounding of hooves.

"No. No. Nooooo." That last sounded close, and she'd have sworn she smelled blood.

She paused and waited for the thunder to near. She caught the wild gaze behind the goggles as the hunter bore down on her. With one hand holding the reins, he aimed a gun with the other.

It never fired. A large red shape leaped from the forest, and the man went down so quickly he didn't make a sound before he died.

The riderless horse pounded past, and she waited.

The big red hybrid straightened, a truly mixed blend of both fox and wolf, the differences subtle and stark at once—the narrower muzzle, the ruddy color of his coat. Beautiful in her eyes.

And she would show him how beautiful, but first...

Yip. She spoke to him.

He cocked his head, bared a fang. *Yap.*

They heard a voice in the distance. He eyed her

and tilted his head, the gesture questioning, *Shall we?*

Indeed, they should. With others in the fur, they hunted by the dawning light until the hunters were gone. As in *gone*, probably never to be found, because Kit knew where to dump the bodies. The same place Gerard had probably used before, a gorge that tightened as it deepened. Not that they stayed to join in the cleanup. One hunter still remained.

Gerard had left a bloody trail. He tried to drive off, but he didn't make it far, as Kit startled him off the road by jumping out when he saw the headlights.

Still, Gerard didn't give up. He spilled out of the vehicle, more meat than man, one side of his face and body a bloody mess. His arm hung limp, chewed and useless. Still, the man refused to cede, limping into the woods.

There was a pleasure in doing the slow stalk after him, knowing he couldn't escape, smelling his fear.

Poppy shifted and drawled, "Leaving so soon? But the hunt's not done yet. Only one more to go."

The level of fear in Gerard sprang a few notches as he whirled to face her, a blubbering mess. "Don't. Please. I'll give you anything."

"Can you give me my womb back? Kit's family?

My mother? The lives of those you killed?" she hissed.

"I—"

She had no use for excuses. She advanced on him, and he fell, landing on his back. His one good hand rose with a gun. *Her* fucking gun, of all things.

His hand shook as he aimed. Fired. And missed. She wrestled the gun from his grip and placed the muzzle against his forehead before discharging it. He died instantly, but she still fired another bullet. Double tap.

This time, she made sure he'd never come back.

TWENTY-SEVEN

Kɪᴛ ᴅɪᴅɴ'ᴛ ʀᴇᴍᴇᴍʙᴇʀ ᴍᴜᴄʜ ᴀғᴛᴇʀ ʙᴇɪɴɢ forced to shift, other than it had involved death and blood. Not his or that of his kind. He'd hunted humans. And enjoyed it, especially the part where his mate had partnered with him.

Together, he and Penny had handled the threat to them and their people. Made the world a safer place. Ended an era of pain and suffering.

Gerard wouldn't be coming back to life this time.

He shifted back and staggered, not just because of exhaustion. It was truly over.

Penny caught his swaying frame. "Kit!"

He hugged her back and buried his face in her hair. He'd thought while in that cage he'd never get to hold her again. "Thank fuck you're safe. Please tell me he didn't hurt you." He didn't scent any injuries, but still...

"I'm fine. You, on the other hand, don't look so good."

"I'm all right. Just hungry and tired."

"Oh hell no. The H word is not allowed around me. No way. Uh-uh." She shook her head.

Wrong thing to say? Or was that the right thing? Because his mate managed to not only get him inside, wrapped in a robe and sitting in a kitchen chair, but she began cooking.

Somehow, soup appeared, a thin broth to start, which, once he had a bite, led to him clearing the bowl while dipping toasted bread. He felt a thousand times better, but when he would have risen to offer help, Penny whirled and menaced him with a flipper.

"Sit. Eat." It seemed better to obey.

He indulged in the piles of pancakes. Juice. Eggs. Drooled when he finished the meal with flan.

Penny worked a magic he'd never seen in that kitchen, the homey scents drawing the Were survivors, one by one. They came in mostly quiet, apprehensive. Then ravenous. They fell on the food, and as their bellies filled, their lips loosened, and stories emerged, haunting recollections of their capture.

It brought them together in a way that made Kit feel less alone. They would forever be scarred by this event, and yet, looking at Penny, he knew if they all had just an ounce of her strength, they'd survive.

One person he didn't see, though. No, make that two people.

He carried his empty plate to the dishwasher and asked Penny in passing, "Where's Luna and Lochlan?"

"Your mom went all Bigfoot Queen Kong and chased Lochlan into the woods."

He blinked. "That couldn't have been Luna. She doesn't shift." Because of a trauma in her youth.

"She did. Not on purpose. Gerard blew some kind of powder at her that made her transform into a crazy-looking wolf. Although I should add I was still pretty drugged at the time. Anyhow, I'm not the only one who saw it. Hammer saw Lochlan leading her away from the house and everyone."

"Um, shouldn't we be looking for them?"

She shook her head. "According to one of the survivors, it's best to let the madness fade, because a forced shift of that sort is a dangerous thing."

"Aren't you worried about Lochlan, then?"

She snorted. "Please. He's tougher than your mom."

"If he hurts her..."

"Lochlan would chew off his own arm first. Don't worry. If anyone can keep her from getting hurt, it's him."

It wasn't the answer Kit wanted. Not when it came to the woman he owed his life to.

Penny cupped his cheeks. "If they're not back in the next hour, we'll go find them."

By the time they did, all they found was a note where the SUV had been parked.

Don't trust the Lykosium. Hide. See you soon.

Scrawled in Luna's handwriting. Ominous, especially with the survivors looking to Kit and Penny for answers.

He had none. But he did have access to a shit-ton of vehicles. Enough for everyone to drive comfortably.

Darian was the one to announce the plan to the others after Kit had explained the situation. They left after lunch, everyone grabbing as much food, clothes, and shit to pawn as they could stuff in their vehicles.

Kit and Penny remained behind to do one last thing.

"Care to do the honors?" he asked, offering her the lighter he'd found. They'd already run a trail of oil from the bottom step into the house.

They'd waited until sunset for this moment so no

one in the distance would see the smoke and come to investigate.

Still, the flame seemed bright as it zipped for the house. They stood side by side, watching as flames engulfed the house of horrors for the last time.

Penny turned into his arms. Shivering. He held her.

"It's over." They said it together and joined their lips as if they were in sync. He devoured her mouth, tasting her, savoring. So sweet. Perfect.

Mine.

He sat her on the hood of the Range Rover they'd kept for themselves, yanking at her loose pants. She shoved at his, freeing his hard cock and gripping it one-handed. She guided him into her, sighing with pleasure as the walls of her sex gripped him. He seated himself fully into her, loving how she pulsed.

She dug her fingers into his shoulders as he thrust into her, the heat of the burning house at his back, though nothing compared to the inferno between them.

She keened and shuddered as she reached her peak. He held her tight, his hips pistoning, getting that angle that caused her sharp cries. He hit it again and again until she clenched him like a vise.

She came. He came. It was that fucking simple. Perfect.

And only she could make him laugh by saying as they cuddled afterward, "I could really go for a roasted marshmallow right about now. I've a bag and some skewers in the trunk if you want to join me."

They ate perfectly browned marshmallows and some crispy ones. They fucked again before getting on the road.

Time to go home.

EPILOGUE

HOME WASN'T THE SAME, POPPY SOON REALIZED, and it wasn't just because of all the new people at the ranch.

She'd changed. Given the cramped conditions, she'd jumped at the invitation when Kit had asked a day after their arrival if she wanted to join him on a trip to Montana so he could take care of some business.

She almost didn't go, given Astra was ready to burst. The baby would come anytime now.

But Astra had said, "Get out of here. I'll call you when my first contraction starts. They say the first time takes forever, meaning you'll have plenty of time to meet me at the hospital. We're leaving in the morning ourselves. Bellamy isn't taking any chances since the baby is still breech."

With that kind of permission, she hadn't been able to resist, although she did wonder at Kit's business. "When are you going to tell me where we are going?"

He'd been awfully cagey about it, offering only one clue. *It's my biggest secret.*

She had to know.

They arrived at a large house that had an old-country vibe to it, from the gray stone to the many peaked roofs that showed the many additions. Trees bloomed all over, and some toys littered the ground.

"What is this place?"

Kit parked and drummed his fingers on the wheel. "How I fought the nightmares."

A woman emerged from the front door, proud of bearing, her hair still mostly dark with a few silver highlights. She was joined by another woman, a bit younger, and a man missing part of a leg.

As Kit emerged from the car, the first woman clapped her hands. "He's brought home his mate."

Home? Poppy eyed the trio, noting the lack of similarity to Kit in appearance. The only thing in common? Were.

"Kit?"

"Trust me." He held her hand as he tugged her forward. "Hi, Irene. Jon. Jenna. How have things been?"

"Oh, you know. Busy. Thanks for getting that sewing machine. It's already come in handy."

"I'm working on getting that loom you asked for too."

Poppy's curiosity deepened.

"Where's the horde?" he asked, glancing left and right, as if looking for someone.

"Here."

The one word might have seemed ominous without the laughter.

It also acted as a signal. Bodies flew from everywhere, some small, others gangly. The kids hit Kit and clung tight, yelling many versions of "Gotcha!" Some not in English.

As Poppy neared, she couldn't help but smile at the littlest one who toddled from behind a bush, hands sticky from the berries she'd mashed into her mouth. She waggled a messy hand, and Kit snared the toddler and tolerated a sloppy kiss.

Poppy arched a brow. "Did you just bring me home to meet all your kids?"

"More like siblings. We're all brothers and sisters here," he said, his free hand reaching down to smooth the curls of a boy clamped to his leg, a thumb tucked in his mouth.

"Hi." She waved, which resulted in the berry

baby reaching out her arms. Poppy never hesitated to scoop up the tiny body. This child was too young to remember, so she easily trusted, but Poppy saw the flight instinct in the other gazes and noticed the guarded way they held themselves. She knew where these children had come from, even the adults standing on the steps. These were the ones Kit had saved who had nowhere to go. They'd had no one to care for them, so he did.

He cared for them all.

She'd never loved him more, because not only had he guided her back to living a full life but he'd given her the one thing she'd thought she'd never have.

The chance to be a mother.

Which came with raspberry fingerprints, she discovered when Tabitha finally let go.

Poppy proudly wore that shirt with the stains every chance she got.

SHE WOKE in the back seat of a car, head pounding, mouth pasty.

Pushing up, she noticed the driver had a rugged profile, his hair salt-and-pepper like his beard.

"Who are you? Where are you taking me?" she asked, putting a hand to her brow for a rub.

He flicked a gaze at her in the rearview. "About time you woke."

"Who are you? For that matter, who am I?"

"You shouldn't drink if you're going to black out."

"I was drinking?" That sounded wrong. She would have sworn she never overindulged.

"We both were after the wedding."

"What wedding?"

His grim reply? "Ours."

WHAT DID LUNA DO? How the heck did she end up married to Lochlan? Find out in *Rogue Unloved.*

FOR MORE INFO on this book or more Eve Langlais titles, please visit, EveLanglais.com.

Made in the USA
Coppell, TX
05 September 2022

82642144R00128